The Bright One

The Bright Series, Volume 1

T. J. Fier

Published by T. J. Fier, 2024.

THE BRIGHT ONE

First edition. September 30, 2024.

ISBN: 979-8227997357

Written by T. J. Fier.

To my first reader, Jarod.

Chapter One

ALEXA BAXTER EXITED River View High School into a sea of boisterous students, jostled from all sides as teenagers headed to after-school activities or their vehicles in the parking lot. She readjusted her headphones, cranked up Nirvana, and tried to make the world disappear.

She paused at the edge of the flow and turned her face to the sun. The rain-soaked morning had turned into a lovely afternoon. Why go home and bury herself in a book when she could head out to her favorite park and try out her new set of drawing pencils? Alexa double-checked if she had all the necessary supplies and hurried to her car.

"Ugh, when did it turn so nice out?" Alexa's bestie, Mateo, lounged on the hood of her worn-out Honda Civic. "I can't believe I have to go to work."

Despite the daily chaos of the high school parking lot, they managed to park side by side every morning.

"Poor baby." Alexa stifled a grin. "Latte Da is such a cruel mistress, isn't she?"

"The worst." Mateo stuck out his tongue as he ran a hand through his chunky bleached highlights. "Where you off to? Listening to sad boy music while re-reading *Wuthering Heights*?"

"Seems like the perfect afternoon to break in a new sketchbook." Alexa nudged her backpack with an elbow. "I might head up to Birkmose."

"Draw me something pretty." Mateo gave Alexa a parting hug and bounced into his idling sedan.

Alexa shouted her goodbyes, blowing Mateo goofy kisses. Her friend caught each one as he pulled out of his parking space. Alexa followed his lead, winding her Civic through the tangle of vehicles and adolescents. Tension slipped from her shoulders as she drove into Riverview's winding streets and well-manicured neighborhoods.

Birkmose Park was seated atop one of the many river bluffs lining the St. Croix River. Her Civic's engine complained as they crested the steep road leading to the park. Alexa whispered promises of a fresh oil change and a new air filter once they found a parking spot.

When she opened her door, birds sang, flitting from tree to tree. Wind-tossed leaves skittered across the parking lot. The breeze from the valley below delivered the damp tang of rotting foliage and the bite of the cold autumn river. The sun was warm, but early October's icy fingers still hung in the shadows. Alexa wound a black scarf around her neck and headed toward her usual picnic table nestled beside an enormous oak tree--her preferred drawing subject.

Alexa settled onto the dusty wood plank seats and piled her drawing supplies on the table. She opened a fresh, unblemished page in her sketchbook, plucked a 2B pencil from the tray, and surveyed her drawing subject one more time before deciding today was a great day to practice leaves.

"Okay, let's do this." Alexa slid her headphones over her ears, hit play on her favorite 90's grunge playlist, and let her pencil run wild.

Bang!

The scrape and tumble of something rattling around the park bathroom to her right knocked her out of her reverie. Alexa slid back one of her headphones. What the heck was that? She waited a moment for someone to come out of the bathroom. The concrete block building stood silent.

"Whatever." Alexa shrugged and returned to her work. Sound had a weird way of bouncing around river valleys. This wouldn't be the first time a shout from the river below managed to make its way up to her perch at the top of the bluff.

The tip of her pencil careened across the drawing paper. Her art teacher always preached to lay out the drawing and worry about details later. Nirvana's "Smells Like Teen Spirit" transitioned into the Smashing Pumpkins' "Bullet with Butterfly Wings" as her drawing gained shape and depth. A few rough curves became the outline of a branch, and a clutter of haphazard lines turned into a cluster of leaves.

Bang! Bang! Screech!

The noise was loud enough to cut through the song's raging chorus. Alexa flinched, nearly ruining her drawing. She paused her music as Billy Corgan was about to let out a primal scream and scanned the park.

Seriously, what the hell was that? Did the racket come from the women's bathroom, of all places? She knew from experience that the women's bathroom held two worse-for-wear stalls and a dribbling sink. The cleanliness was questionable, especially at this time of year, so she typically avoided using the park's lavatory at all costs.

Caught in the familiar, obsessive need to finish rendering the oak branch, she returned to her drawing. The sketch would be ruined if she didn't complete the shadows before the light changed.

Yet another series of booms and bangs radiated from the women's bathroom. The noise startled her this time, sending her pencil in a dark arc across her sketchbook. Alexa let out a series of foul words, tossed aside her pencil, and slammed the sketchbook shut. Her artistic impulses were crushed—time to investigate what was making all the fuss.

The noisemaker had to be some kind of animal. Probably a big one. Alexa scanned the backlog of her brain for the beasts of Riverview and came up with the shortlist: dog, deer, or maybe a bear. Hadn't her mother mentioned a black bear spotted in downtown Riverview only a week ago? Or was that somewhere else in Wisconsin?

She texted Mateo, *R there bears in Riverview?*

Sure. Or do you mean bears that live in the woods? He replied.

Alexa rolled her eyes. *Bears that live in THE WOODS. Have you seen one before?*

Hell no. You know I'm allergic to pine trees. He added emojis of a person running and a bear. *According to Google, if you see a bear, you're supposed to get really big and yell.*

Alexa typed a series of panicked emoji faces, sent off her message, and waited to see if the trapped creature would start banging around again.

Nothing. It may be time to head home anyway. Clouds had gathered on the horizon, smothering the beautiful shadows once cast by the oak tree. Her drawing was ruined, and so was her opportunity to start again.

Yet another hollow bang echoed from the bathroom, this time followed by a weak and half-hearted cry. Something was stuck in there and Alexa needed to help it. She jumped to her feet, smoothed the front of her black ZERO t-shirt, rearranged her stocking cap, and crept toward the bathroom.

The cinder block building was still damp from the morning rain. The smell of disinfectant and urine hit Alexa as she approached the ladies' room door. An unnatural halo of dead grass surrounded the building's foundation. She toed the moldering turf. How weird.

Alexa drew close to the door and attempted to be as quiet as possible. She didn't want to scare whatever was stuck in there. Pressing her ear to the door, she could hear heavy, uneven breathing on the other side. A fresh cry of defeat echoed, similar to the one from minutes before. She counted down from ten, heaved a fortifying breath, and yanked open the door.

"I'm-I'm coming in," slipped from Alexa's lips before she had time to think better of it. The animal wouldn't understand her, of course, but uttering the words settled her nerves.

At first, the bathroom appeared as expected—dark and dreary compared to the honeyed light outside. A single bare bulb lit the grim space. Alexa rubbed her arms, holding them tight to her body. A chill drifted under her t-shirt and shivered down her back.

Standing in the bleak space, she could hear the soft scraping of something on concrete. A faint panting drifted from the accessible stall. Alexa tiptoed further in and dropped to a crouch. Between the gaps beneath the stalls, she counted four blond cloven hooves standing on the damp floor.

Was it a goat? How the heck did a goat get all the way in there? Or maybe it was a deer? Did deer have white legs with little tufts of hair curling around their ankles?

The deer-goat's front hooves lifted off the floor. A wail shook from the back stall. Alexa clapped her hands over her ears. The sound was unlike anything she had heard before, like the screech of a cat combined with a horse's trumpeting whinny. The creature hurled itself against the stall, hooves scrambling for purchase. The sound of metal tearing covered Alexa's pathetic shriek.

The racket faded as quickly as it began. Alexa pressed a fist to her mouth, heart thrumming. She considered bolting and calling the local police, leaving the poor trapped creature behind.

Instead, for once in her life, she decided to be brave.

"Hello?" she called out.

Alexa tiptoed around the first bathroom stall. The accessible stall door hung open, sagging on its bent hinges. A dozen small hoof-sized dents had turned the door into a crumpled ruin. The milky pale flanks of the deer-goat finally appeared—time to get a proper look at the poor thing.

Alexa gasped. "No way."

She coughed, catching herself against the door frame before her knees buckled. The trapped animal wasn't a goat or a deer. No, nothing so ordinary.

"Holy shit."

The beast flicked a lion-like tail with a cascading plume of white hair long enough to reach the floor. Its hair shimmered fine as silk threads, and light refracted off flaxen curls. Radiant blue eyes stared back at her with a mixture of fear and defiance.

Alexa's head seemed to disconnect from her body, unable to process what stood before her. She refused to accept the creature and backed away, her hearing racing. A sensation passed through her head as if something stuck between her ears suddenly loosened. Her head ached from the shift, and panic tingled down her spine.

The faint light couldn't manipulate the shape she had seen nor change the animal into anything other than what stood before her.

It was a unicorn.

A real.

Live.

Freaking unicorn.

Chapter Two

A UNICORN?

Alexa turned the word over in her head. Such a ridiculous word. She shoved open the door to the adjacent bathroom stall. The unicorn's silver-gold spiral of a horn had punched through the steel walls and tangled into the remnants of the toilet paper dispenser.

"Oh, shit," she giggled. "I'm losing my mind."

Her legs gelatinized beneath her as she slumped onto the floor.

Alexa had never witnessed a miraculous thing before. She had an ordinary, middle-class suburban life with her parents and annoying sister. They had a lovely house and lived in a nice neighborhood. Sure, Alexa was a little more eccentric than the rest of her family, but discovering a unicorn trapped in a Birkmose Park bathroom stall was the last way she expected to spend her Monday afternoon.

Staring at the opalescent horn of the magical creature, she performed mental cartwheels to justify its existence. Was she losing her mind? Did someone slip hallucinogens into the school water supply as a joke?

Please. I need you to help me!

A small, thin voice slinked through Alexa's head. She flinched, staggered away from the tangled unicorn horn, and stood outside the two open bathroom stalls. Did she hear something, or was her brain trying to sort out an impossible situation? Frozen in place, unsure of what she ought to do, the urge to giggle once again tickled the base of her throat.

The unicorn's chest rose, fell, and released a defeated sigh. The impossible creature was similar in size to the white-tailed deer that lived in the woods near Alexa's home. Its withers were roughly the same height as her waist. The poor beast had braced its body at an awkward angle against the stall dividers, front legs splayed apart. The unicorn's head—a mixture between a horse and a deer—was shoved against the stall's side.

Alexa pitied the awkward arrangement but did not know how to help. The unicorn studied Alexa. Its gaze sparked with fiery intelligence. The beast seemed to be determining whether Alexa was a friend or foe.

Their eyes connected. A peculiar pulse shot through Alexa's chest. The probing sensation slid from her heart to the back of her neck. Then, the strange feeling sank into the front of her skull, released another throb, and settled there. She didn't move an inch while it happened, truly worried if she was losing her mind or having some sort of stroke.

Alexa rubbed her forehead. "What the heck just happened?"

Please. I need you to help me, Alexa Baxter, said the whisper of a voice echoing within her skull.

"Who? What? How do you know my name?" she stammered, slapping her hands over her ears. "How can I hear you?"

I heard your name when I surveyed your brain's faculties. That is why you can listen to me at this moment.

"My *brain*? Is that what I felt? How did you—"

I need your help, Alexa Baxter.

Alexa slumped against the wall at her back. "You want me to help you?"

The unicorn snorted. *Yes, please. As you can see, I am quite trapped.*

"Trapped?"

Indeed, Alexa Baxter.

"Oh, right. Yeah, your horn thingy is in the toilet dispenser. How did you—"

Can you help me?

"Yes?"

Excellent. Let us proceed.

"What should I do?" Alexa straightened, pushing aside the childlike giddiness trembling through her fingers. She swallowed another giggle.

We must release me from this entanglement. You must push my horn while I pull, Alexa Baxter, said the wind voice, which was neither masculine nor feminine in tone.

Alexa glanced into the neighboring stall and surveyed the twisting mass of metal and toilet paper. The unicorn's horn was a shining piece of broken sunlight among the fray. "Oh, boy."

Can you do it? The unicorn fluttered dark lashes tipped with gold.

"I'll sure try." Alexa squared her shoulders and returned to the adjacent stall. She studied the toilet dispenser twisted around the unicorn's horn and gave it a tentative tug. The metal bent without too much effort.

"Ok, give me a second." She peeled back the aluminum sections like the petals of a flower. A couple of shards remained impossibly curled around the horn, but at least she now had space for her hands.

Grasp my horn and push with all your strength.

Alexa's graphite-smeared hands fluttered near the horn. "Are you sure? What if I hurt you?"

You cannot hurt me. I am stronger than I look, but I cannot do this without your help, Alexa Baxter.

"What if I break your horn?" Despite her mounting fear, Alexa gripped the horn as tight as possible. The spiraling edge had an unexpected serrated texture and bit into her skin. The horn was warm in her hands.

That is not possible. Now, are you ready?

"Okay, yes, sure. I'll count to three, and then I'll push, and you'll pull?" Alexa shouted. Her voice shook and reached a dog-whistle pitch as she realized what she was about to do. She took a deep breath, braced herself, and said, "On three. One. Two. Three!"

Alexa poured every stitch of strength her petite body could muster and pushed. A determined grunt came from the unicorn as it bucked in the adjacent stall. It seemed as if the horn wouldn't budge for a moment, but then, with a great shriek of metal, the horn slipped from her hands. Alexa watched as the unicorn fall into a sprawling heap through the remaining hole.

"We did it!"

The unicorn rolled onto its side and untangled its legs. With an irritated snort, the mythical creature found its footing and heaved itself back onto its cloven feet. The unicorn shook and blew another breath, tail switching whip-like against its milky flanks.

"You okay?" Alexa exited the stall, still unable to believe what stood before her.

My back and neck are stiff, but I am otherwise unharmed. The unicorn turned and—led by the spiral of its horn—exited the stall. The beast took a lengthy assessment of Alexa as its withers twitched. Light danced and fractured off the creature's shimmering coat: a diamond stuck in the mud.

Where am I, Alexa Baxter? The unicorn huffed and let out a graceful sneeze.

"A bathroom?" Alexa replied, heart pounding a wild rhythm. "How is this real? Oh, my God. Mateo will never believe this."

What are the gods here? The unicorn turned its piercing gaze upon her.

"What?" Alexa balked, the question hardly making sense to her rattled brain. "Well, some people believe in one god, I guess? But, that really depends on which religion—"

And what sort of god? Sun? Thunder? Earth? The unicorn demanded. *Omnipotent? Tempestuous?*

"I guess it depends on who you're talking to?"

The unicorn tossed its head as if unsatisfied by her answers. The creature stomped a delicate hoof. *I do not understand, Alexa Baxter. Where am I?*

"Wisconsin? Well, Riverview, Wisconsin, if you want to be more specific."

I do not know this ... Wisconsin. The unicorn heaved a great sigh. *I did not mean to come here. I have made a grave error.*

"Well, you must know the United States, of course. Right? Though, you don't sound like you come from around here. That accent—"

The United States? Is that the name of this world? What class of planet am I treading upon?

"World?" Alexa's eyes grew wide. Could it be possible the unicorn wasn't from Earth? If so, how did it get here? She had heard about other dimensions in physics class, but all that seemed so theoretical. "Have you heard of Earth?"

The unicorn laid back its ears and snorted. *Earth. I see. How very unfortunate.*

The unicorn wasn't from Earth? Did that make the unicorn an alien? Of all the things Alexa expected to do on a Monday afternoon, meeting an alien unicorn was the least possible.

Very well. The unicorn pointed its pink snout toward the bathroom exit. *Please open the door for me, Alexa Baxter. I cannot stand to spend another moment in this foul place.*

"Oh, yeah. Sure. Okay."

Reaching to grab the door handle, Alexa noticed a sharp stinging sensation across her palms. She turned one over to find razor-thin scratch marks covering her palms and weeping delicate beads of blood. A fat drop dripped from her thumb and spattered onto the floor.

The horn's serrated edges had cut her when she helped the unicorn free itself from the toilet dispenser. She hadn't noticed before. Hardly a surprise, she barely knew how to move her legs as the unicorn tapped an impatient hoof against the door.

"My hands." Alexa turned her bleeding palms to the alien creature.

Apologies, Alexa Baxter. The unicorn said in an unapologetic tone. *After you free me, you must bandage that up.*

Alexa pulled the sleeve of her cardigan over her right hand. The ruined skin throbbed in response. It was a good thing she loved wearing black. She might be able to wash the sweater before her mother noticed the stain.

Wincing, Alexa opened the bathroom door and let the unicorn out into the warm, gleaming sunlight.

Chapter Three

THE UNICORN'S SPLENDOR blinded Alexa as it leaped into the sunlight. Tail twitching, neck arched, the magnificent beast pranced across the park's fading green turf. The unicorn surveyed the park, ears flicking in multiple directions as it listened to the various and perhaps strange surroundings.

I was told Earth was a wild, dangerous planet. The deer-sized creature nosed the wind. *The reports may have been exaggerated.*

Alexa stared at the dazzling creature until her eyes ached. She turned away as more blood dripped from her bleeding hands.

"Hey, is there anything you can do about this?" Alexa turned her palms in the unicorn's direction.

Do something? The unicorn snorted. *I am confused. What do you expect me to do?*

"Can't you magically fix them or something?" Alexa whimpered and pulled the sleeves of her sweater over her torn hands.

Magic? I do not know this word. What is magic? Alexa Baxter, you ask very odd questions.

"Well, you're a unicorn, right? In the stories, unicorns are magical ... and stuff."

Alexa Baxter, what in the worlds is a unicorn? Have you injured your brain as well as your hands?

Alexa's throat tightened. "Aren't you a unicorn?"

Magic. Unicorn. I do not understand these words. All of this overwhelms me. The unicorn's ears drooped as it once more scanned the park. *I should have never come this way. What have I done?*

Alexa's phone vibrated in her back pocket. How many notifications has she missed? Did it matter? Mateo would want to know all about her adventure in the park. She scanned her best friend's unanswered texts: *So, was it a bear? Did you find it? Please tell me you aren't bringing it home with you.*

She types out a bloody *BRB*, knowing Mateo would only send her another flurry of texts.

Meanwhile, the unicorn trotted across the park, continuing to flick its ears in every direction. It shied at the sound of a semi's air brakes from the interstate and squealed when a plastic bag drifted across the parking lot.

Alexa's vision blurred. She bent forward and took a deep, cleansing breath, curling her hands into fists to keep from bleeding all over her jeans. She ought to go home, bandage her hands, and then decide what to do about the unicorn loping across Birkmose Park.

Hadn't her mother stuffed gloves into her backpack that morning when the temperature hovered a little too close to freezing? Dazed, she shuffled over to her forgotten backpack, which was still on the picnic table, along with her drawing supplies. With her blood-dripping fingers, she pulled out the set of black knit gloves stuffed in the front pocket. She sucked air through her teeth, sliding the dark fabric over the bloody mess. The pain made her vision slide sideways, so she dropped her butt onto the picnic table's bench and continued to take deep, centering breaths.

The unicorn, who wasn't a unicorn, continued exploring the park. Alexa rechecked her phone, ignored Mateo's seven additional texts, and noted the time. Already after five. Had she been there for almost two hours? The sun has sunk further towards the horizon. She needed to get home before the rest of her family to clean up and figure out what to do with the unicorn.

What did one do with a unicorn?

She couldn't leave the lost creature behind, especially if it was from another world. Could animal control help? Maybe the police? No, that didn't feel right either. Alexa was far from the ideal person to help an alien unicorn, but there was no one else.

"I think I need to hide you somewhere," Alexa said as the unicorn circled back from its investigation of the park.

Hide? Is that necessary? The unicorn turned in the direction of the interstate, flaring its nostrils. *I must leave at once. I do not belong on this planet. I have come in the wrong direction.*

"How about I take you home, and maybe we can figure out what to do from there?"

Home? How can taking me to your home help? I have heard about the savagery of Earth inhabitants. What do you mean to do to me?

"I just want to help you," Alexa shouted.

There is no need to raise your voice, Alexa Baxter.

Her head was such a mixed-up mess. She didn't know what to process first. She needed to get the unicorn out of the park and somehow take it to a safe place so they could sort out how or if she could help. As she gathered her sketchbook and pencils, an idea came to mind.

"I think I know where to put you. You're not safe here. Who knows what someone else would do if they found you? Probably post a video on TikTok or worse. You know, you're only about the size of my aunt's Great Dane..."

Alexa moved as if in a dream to her car. She opened the doors to the back seats, hands quivering, gloves stiffened with her drying blood. She moved the passenger-side seat as far up as it would go and turned back to the unicorn, who had cocked its head and watched her with cautious interest. It glimmered like a sunburst in the fading afternoon light.

"Yeah, we'll need to do something about that."

Opening her trunk, Alexa scanned the contents. Her mother had shoved gloves into her backpack and tossed in winter weather emergency gear in her trunk. Alexa giggled when she found what she was looking for: a flannel king-sized blanket, perfect for hiding an otherworldly, sparkly unicorn in her back seat.

Alexa slammed the trunk closed. "We have a storage shed in our backyard. My family barely goes in and out of it this time of year. There are plenty of places to hide you until we decide what to do next."

The unicorn switched its tail. The beast surveyed the tight but manageable back seat and then turned its piercing eyes upon her. *Do you mean for me to get in that?*

"This is all I got."

The unicorn let out yet another long, weary sigh. *Very well. I will go with you, Alexa Baxter.*

"Great. Let's get you in the back."

The unicorn fit unexpectedly well in the back seat, curled up like a dog with its head tucked over its front legs. The tip of its horn dug into the back of the Civic's passenger seat and left a sizable puncture wound behind. How would she explain that to her parents? Who cared? She was taking home a unicorn.

"So, I'm going to cover you up with this blanket so you don't freak people out on the way home. You're just—uh—really sparkly."

I am at your mercy, Alexa Baxter. You know your kind much better than I do.

In a state of disbelief, Alexa draped the blanket over the unicorn, and the fabric covered everything but the tip of the beast's opalescent horn. Good enough for driving across town.

"Ok, don't move around too much and we should be fine." Alexa dropped into the driver's seat. As long as she couldn't see the unicorn in her rearview mirror, she might be able to concentrate on the road. No one would have guessed by looking at her, but Alexa was an excellent driver. In fact, it was one of her few places of confidence in life.

This is almost comfortable. Thank you, Alexa Baxter.

At least the unicorn was polite. Alexa snapped her seatbelt into place and turned the ignition key. She grew hyper-aware of every action, every gesture she made, from the jagged edge to her breathing to the gentle roar of the Civic's engine. One of Alexa's many playlists blasted over her speakers.

"Sorry about that." Alexa turned down the volume, trying to ignore the mounting pain in her hands.

What was that horrible noise? The unicorn's head rose beneath the blanket.

"The Butthole Surfers. You know, 'I don't mind the sun sometimes.' Oh, no. I bet you haven't heard them before."

Surfer? Butthole? Earth is so bizarre.

"Yeah, I suppose so," Alexa agreed and checked her blind spot three times to ensure all was clear despite being the only vehicle in the park. "It'll only take ten minutes to get to my house. I'm driving a unicorn to my house. Holy shit. Okay. Let's do this."

Alexa eased her car out of the parking spot, mumbling curses as she gripped the steering wheel. The pain was worth the treasure she carried in her backseat. As she drove through Riverview, she tried to ignore the sparkle of the unicorn's horn every time she glanced in the rearview mirror.

Chapter Four

TEN MINUTES LATER, Alexa and the unicorn crept into her backyard. Her parent's enormous privacy fence provided excellent shelter from the neighbor's prying eyes. Even now, Alexa's mind continued to doubt what her eyes beheld.

Mateo would never believe it. He had sent her six additional texts since she tucked the unicorn into her backseat. She finally replied via voice text: *Hang on, super busy.* He answered with a meme of a kitten hanging from a tree branch.

Where have you brought me, Alexa Baxter? Half-covered in the plaid blanket, the unicorn crept along the fence line. Alexa couldn't help but quiver each time the unicorn silently spoke her name, even if the beast's tone was filled with weary impatience.

"My backyard. Dad likes his privacy. That's also why we kept so many trees in our yard."

Tree? Is this a tree? The unicorn knocked a hoof against the nearest sugar maple. *Is it dying? Its foliage withers and falls.*

"No, this is what our trees do in the autumn." Alexa's heart fluttered. "You don't have trees where you come from?"

No, not like these. Anyway, did you say something about hiding me, Alexa Baxter?

"Yeah. The shed's over here."

The pole barn was unused most of the fall, but there was always a chance Alexa's dad might pull out a rake to gather an errant fallen leaf. For the unicorn's sake, she was willing to take a chance. With a heave and grunt, Alexa pulled open the shed's door. She peered into the murk, inhaling the familiar smell of dust, earth, and motor oil.

"This is it." Alexa waved through the open door. She surveyed the collection of distorted shadows and wondered if the strange surroundings might scare the unicorn.

The unicorn flicked its eyes across the yard and flinched when a furious blue jay flew past. *What a horrible flying beast.*

"Don't worry, no birds in here." Alexa entered the shed and hit the light switch. The familiar arrangement of recreational gear, lawn-care items, and random boxes packed the space. The shed was almost full, from her family's pedal bikes and her dad's boat to the riding lawnmower.

Is this our best option, Alexa Baxter? The unicorn stretched out its neck and sniffed at her mother's mountain bike. *Am I safe here?*

"Perfectly safe. There's some room behind the boat." Alexa gestured to the nook beneath the outboard motor. She would have to rearrange a few things to conceal the unicorn properly. "I can find some old blankets to make it comfortable. But, at least for now, this is our best option."

Then, I must make the best of the situation. The unicorn sniffed the handlebars of a nearby bike and sneezed. The creature flattened its ears and inelegantly coughed, exposing a pale blue tongue. *Such an odd world this is.*

"How did you end up here? If you don't mind me asking?" Alexa studied the unicorn's every move.

I am running from a monster, the unicorn said as it examined a row of hanging lawn care equipment.

"A monster?" Alexa squeaked. Monsters were real? Well, if unicorns were real, then so could monsters. Right? "I mean, are you serious? Why is it after you?"

It is a complicated situation, Alexa Baxter. Best you only know some of the details.

"Complicated?" Alexa's mind raced with a thousand questions. "Am I in danger? If a monster is after you, would it come after me, too? I don't want—"

No, Alexa Baxter. The monster would barely notice you or your kind. They only want one thing. Me.

"Whoa." She leaned against the boat to steady herself. Her head buzzed. The repeated need to giggle returned. "How long before—"

I left the monster far behind me—for now. They will find me if I stay too long. Night approaches, and as I do not know this world, I must make the best of the situation. I have been trapped in worse places.

"Yeah, they really need to take better care of those bathrooms."

Indeed. Quite revolting. My name is Una.

"Oh, that's a nice name."

I must continue to ask for your help. Will you continue to help me, Alexa Baxter?

"I—I—ugh, yeah. Sure. I'll try." How dare she refuse the demands of a unicorn? She gnawed on her bottom lip. What did a unicorn need to thrive? All those years watching National Geographic documentaries wouldn't help her now.

Excellent. Now, could you find me a space to rest? I am very weary from my journey.

Alexa nodded in reply and shoved her way through the tumult of storage gear. She squirmed into the space behind the boat and started making space. So, the unicorn had a name. Una. Simple. Direct. Kind of pretty. But what about the monster? When a unicorn escaped from another world, what sort of monster followed? A dragon? Dragons were a journey too far for her already taxed brain, so she pushed the thought aside. The unicorn was enough insanity for one day.

She did her best moving items without using her wounded hands by balancing boxes between her forearms. Unfortunately, she dropped a box labeled "Christmas Decorations" and winced at the sound of glass shattering.

"Here, you can rest on this for now."

The blue plastic tarp Alexa unfolded and spread across the floor crinkled loudly under Una's hooves. The unicorn settled onto the floor with another deep sigh, carefully maneuvering its horn around the surrounding boxes. Once Una rested its total weight on the floor, it took a long breath. Plumes of dust rose from its surroundings.

"Will this be okay?" Alexa leaned around the bowrider. The question wasn't just for the unicorn. Would she be okay? How was she expected to sit down and have dinner with her family while hiding a unicorn in their backyard shed?

Una turned its shining eyes toward her. *For now. Thank you, Alexa Baxter.*

Alexa didn't understand the mechanics behind Una's voice, the pretty words whispering in her head and not in her ears. Weren't there a series of strange sensations when she first met Una? Did the unicorn do something to her? Was that why they could communicate?

"And tomorrow?"

I need to ponder everything that has happened. Then, I will decide what I must do next. Right now, I must rest.

"And I'll do whatever I can to help you." She meant what she said with every inch of her heart.

What she didn't say aloud was the truth: Alexa hadn't seen or done much in the world during her eighteen years in it. She appreciated the relatively sheltered life her parents provided. All they asked of her was to be a good student and get into a good college. She might be, in fact, completely useless.

Thank you, Alexa Baxter. I do not know if I would have ever released myself from that horrible building if you had not set me free. I am in your debt.

Alexa shrugged. "I just did what anyone else would do. No big deal."

Nevertheless, I thank you.

"I'm glad I found you." Alexa's phone buzzed for the hundredth time. "But I gotta go. My family will be home any second, and they know I never come out to the shed. I have a feeling they shouldn't know about you."

Yes, the less they know, the better.

"I'll sneak out some blankets if possible so you won't get cold. Oh, and one more thing. If you're not a unicorn, what are you?"

We are called the Bright Ones.

Chapter Five

"GOD, LEX, WHAT'S WRONG with you?"

Alexa looked up from her plate of spaghetti, fork in her bandaged hand. She had been lost in thought as images of unicorns danced through her head. Or, to be more accurate, a Bright One. The worried faces of her family around the dinner table shook her out of her reverie.

"Huh?" Alexa stabbed her fork into her plate and swirled noodles around the prongs.

"Mom asked you a question, Queen of Darkness." Andrea, Alexa's younger sister, rolled her eyes and smirked.

"Huh?" Alexa repeated and shoveled in a mouthful of spaghetti. Chewing gave her time to think and formulate an answer.

Pretty and blonde, Andrea, a younger reflection of her equally lovely mother, said, "Mom asked what happened to your hands."

Alexa turned to her mother. Cynthia, like many of the high-powered women of Riverview, didn't appear her forty-eight years of age thanks to a routine of Botox, organic vegan living, and hot yoga. The spaghetti noodles Alexa chewed were, of course, gluten-free. What she wouldn't give for some all-purpose flour.

Chewing a thick wad of quinoa pasta, Alexa flexed the mess of bandages wrapped around her hands. The tape around her right hand had already loosened, allowing a peek of the pink, scabbed skin beneath.

Two pairs of similar eyes stared back at Alexa from across the table, one set full of concern, the other annoyance. Alexa's dad, Rodger, the parent she took after, was engrossed with something on his phone. Likely an article from the Wall Street Journal or Forbes. Alexa and Andrea weren't allowed to use their phones at the dinner table, but her dad got away with it.

Alexa swallowed. "I fell."

"*How* did you fall?" Cynthia shook back her shoulder-length blonde hair and sipped her night's allowance of cabernet.

"Tripped."

Andrea pursed her lips. "Lex, just answer the question."

"I was at Birkmose Park and tripped on a rock." Alexa shrugged.

"What were you doing at Birkmose Park?" Cynthia asked, using her "you know I'm a lawyer" tone.

"Homework." Alexa shoved another large forkful of spaghetti into her mouth. She might get through dinner without spilling her guts if she stuck with one-word answers. Picturing Una hiding behind her dad's boat, her fingers trembled. She dropped her fork and stuffed her hands in her lap to hide the evidence.

"How often do you do your homework in the park?" Cynthia frowned.

Alexa swallowed her spaghetti. "Depends."

Cynthia rubbed at her eyebrow. "On what?"

"The weather."

Alexa's parents didn't know how often she went to the park to draw. She squirreled away her growing pile of sketchbooks in her school locker, far from prying parental eyes. They might worry if they knew how far her love for art and drawing truly stretched. Alexa was supposed to become a lawyer, just like her parents. She had let them hold onto that fiction since she first tested in the 99th percentile in kindergarten.

"Well, at least one of you appreciates the great outdoors." Cynthia smiled and cast an exaggerated glare of disappointment toward Andrea.

"Hey, you know how much I hate insects." Andrea held up her hands. "At least I engage in extracurricular activities instead of falling over at a park."

"You just like how good your ass looks in those tiny shorts," Alexa grumbled.

"Language." Cynthia tossed back a large gulp of wine.

"And you're just jealous." Andrea smirked, flipping her long blonde hair behind her shoulder.

"With a body like this, no way." Alexa gestured to her shapeless figure and smirked right back.

"Now, now, you're both pretty," Alexa's father said, not looking up from his phone.

Andrea giggled, and Alexa joined her. They often gave each other a good ribbing but didn't really mean it—at least, not all the time.

"Be more careful in the future, okay?" Alexa's mom said in her Mom Voice, narrowing her eyes over her bulbous wine glass.

"I'll try," Alexa said. She poked at the sauce-smear remains on her plate.

"Yes, listen to your mother." Her father sighed at something he read on his phone and dropped it on the table in disgust. He adjusted the gold-framed glasses, which gave him an air of polished dignity. "So, Alexa, what's the current status of your college applications?"

"Ugh … fine." Alexa shrank in her seat. Must he bring that up at every dinner?

Cynthia said, "Last time I checked, you've already applied to three. Are you working on two more?"

"I finished my fourth application last night." Alexa's face grew hot. When she thought of college, of existence far from her family and everything she knew, fear and joy overtook her in anxiety-filled waves. "Almost done with Macalester."

"She should get her responses by the end of the month." Cynthia nodded to her husband. "But with her grades and test scores, I'm not worried."

"Now, if you had more extra-curriculars, you could have applied to prestigious schools." Rodger adjusted his glasses.

"I know, Dad." Alexa shrunk further into her chair.

"College, for me, was some of the most important years of my life." Rodger pointed his fork at his daughter and took a thoughtful bite.

Alexa and Andrea exchanged a look. Dad had fallen into lecture mode.

"You will form some of the most important networking connections. You need to surround yourself with a high-caliber group of people who can get you the furthest in life. You might be this quiet loner in high school, but you can reset and start over at a good university. Good grades, professors, and people will help you launch a successful career. Just like your mom and I. You need to move on from this whole girl-in-black masquerade."

"Honey, she's just experimenting," Cynthia assured her husband. "There's nothing wrong with a little self-expression at her age."

Alexa crumpled further into her chair. She was subjected to similar conversations at least once a week. Her parents were disappointed their daughter didn't look like she walked out of an L.L. Bean catalog. They were disappointed she didn't have a big gang of friends. And they were disappointed by her shy, reserved nature. In short, they wanted her to be more like Andrea.

"Can I be excused?" Alexa blurted, unable to stand yet another discourse regarding her future state.

Cynthia said, "Rinse your dishes and put them in the dishwasher, please."

Alexa bolted from the table and rinsed her dinner plate in the sink. Her fingers dodged the stream of water. She wasn't up to redressing her wounds after the day she had. Her family continued to murmur behind her as she put her dishes in the dishwasher.

Before her father could go on about her being such a disappointment, she turned and jogged upstairs to the second floor. Her room sat at the end of the hallway, the farthest corner of their sprawling American craftsman house. She grabbed her headphones sitting on her bedstand, grabbed her phone, and lost herself in the roar of Kurt Cobain's immortal angst.

She dropped onto her bed, laden with books, an assortment of art supplies, and a novelty fleece blanket, Frida

Kahlo's *Self Portrait with Thorn Necklace and Hummingbird*. She picked up the nearest textbook and turned to the reading due tomorrow for AP United States History. Sure, she may have discovered the most insane thing possible in the park that afternoon, but she still had a pile of homework and a stream of texts from Mateo to answer.

A figurine on her dresser caught her eye.

Alexa walked over to the acrylic pink-and-purple-haired unicorn sitting atop her chest of drawers. She had taken loving care of the figurine even as a child. Its mane and tail were sleek and straight as the first time she pulled the plastic unicorn from its packaging. Together, they had gone on all sorts of adventures. She used to draw it from every possible angle.

She picked up the miniature unicorn and stood next to her bedroom window. The window looked into their backyard, providing an unobscured view of the shed. Though filled with a secret, the shed told no stories in the dark. Was Una settling in okay? She barely had time to toss the unicorn an old quilt and a few apples before her mom got home. Until her family went to sleep, she didn't dare bother Una.

Instead, she returned to the normalcy of her bedroom and returned to her history textbook. Her phone vibrated. Yet another exasperated text from Mateo. She couldn't put him off any longer.

Sorry, I ghosted, she typed. *Something crazy happened to me at the park, but I have to explain it in person. You'll never believe what I found.*

Chapter Six

ALEXA'S PHONE READ five minutes past six when she crept out the back door and shuffled out to the shed. The morning frost has iced over the lawn, slicking the grass. Bleary from a night of poor sleep, she nearly stumbled twice before reaching the door. Her parents' alarm went off at 6:30 am every morning, so there wasn't much time to see how the unicorn had fared overnight.

If Una existed. Between forcing herself to read through the fourth act of The Seagull for AP Literature and Composition and midnight, Alexa started to wonder if she had made up Una. Was she losing her mind? Unicorns didn't exist. However, all she had to do was flex her hands a couple of times to remember the Bright One in the park must be real. The itching cuts told their own story.

When Alexa did sleep, she dreamed of unicorns, slavering monsters, and rejection letters from colleges. Bird song woke her near dawn. Exhausted but unexpectedly alert, Alexa decided she couldn't leave for school until she checked on Una.

By the time Alexa reached the shed door, shivering in her pajamas, she continued questioning everything that had brought her to that moment. Unicorns? Monsters? Creatures from other worlds? What had happened to her quiet little life?

Giving the door three light raps, she opened it and hurried inside before she lost her nerve. The shed's interior was dark except for a thin slice of light beneath the shed's door.

"Una?" Alexa's shrilled voice echoed through the pole barn. "Hey, are you there? Please be here. Please tell me I'm not losing my—"

The tarp crinkled from behind the boat. Even in the darkness, Alexa swore she could see a glimmer of Una's horn.

Yes, Alexa Baxter. What is happening? Is it time to leave? Have you found me a way off this wretched planet?

Alexa's breath hitched. It hadn't been a dream. Nor was she losing her mind, "No, I wanted to check on you to see … uh … how you slept."

How I slept? On a cold, hard floor, that is how I slept. Alexa Baxter.

"Oh, sorry. I wanted to bring some blankets, but I couldn't. You see, my parents—"

I do not care about your familial circumstances. I need to know what we are doing next. The plastic tarp crackled and snapped as the unicorn must have stumbled to its feet. A body collided against cardboard, sending a stack of metallic clanging to the ground.

"Sshhhh! You gotta be quiet, Una, or my parents—"

A string of angry words Alexa didn't understand rang through her skull. Was the unicorn cursing her out? She finally had the sense to turn on the overhead light, and the unicorn let out a whinny shriek. Una plunged from beneath the outboard engine and staggered into a tower of boxes.

You foolish earth creature! Are you trying to blind me?

"Sorry. I'm so sorry." Alexa slapped a bandaged hand at the light switch, returning them to complete darkness. Alexa wasn't much of a morning person either, but Una's foul mood hit her like a freight train. Where had the beautiful, polite little beast gone?

Una's hooves scuttled across the concrete floor. *That is better, Alexa Baxter. By all that is bright, how my back aches. When do we leave?*

"Leave?" Alexa blinked, unable to see anything as her eyes readjusted to the dark.

Yes, Alexa Baxter. The time has come for me to leave. I have lingered in this place too long.

"I have to go to school in a couple hours."

School? Alexa could hear more shuffling of angry unicorn feet. *Do you mean an educational facility?*

"Yeah, I'm in my senior year of high school. Sorry, I should have mentioned I have to go there today. I would skip, but I'm not really com—"

Are you leaving me here, Alexa Baxter? Alone, with no one to help me?

"Only until this afternoon. Hey, did you want me to grab you some food before my parents—"

Alexa Baxter, this is unacceptable. You must get me out of here. The monster could arrive at any moment.

"And I will. I promise. First, I must go to school and get my friend to help."

Help? I thought you did not trust anyone to know about me.

"You can trust Mateo. He'll know what to do. He always knows what to do." Alexa silently prayed she was right. A unicorn was too big of a project for her alone. She needed the one person she trusted more than anyone else.

Una breathed in soft, irritated puffs that glanced against Alexa's cheeks. When did Una get so close? As Alexa's eyes adjusted to the darkness, she realized the unicorn stood only a couple of feet away; its horn pointed at her heart. Alexa took an instinctive step back, heels bumping into the closed door behind her.

"Una?"

Very well, Alexa Baxter. I will allow you to retrieve this ... help. I beg you not to take too long. I fear the monster could arrive at any moment. We have little time to spare.

"I won't." Alexa's voice wavered. Her heart pounded in her ears. She hadn't considered the unicorn's horn could be brandished like a weapon. Was that what Una had done? Threatening her? "So ... are you hungry?"

No. I do not require nourishment at this time.

"Great. Well, I better get going." Alexa reached for the door handle, which was pressing against her back. "My parents will be up any second, and I don't want them to catch me out here."

Do not fail me, Alexa Baxter. I am counting on you.

"I won't. I promise. Okay, bye." Alexa tugged open the door, relieved to stumble into the icy morning. Her breath caught in her throat, and she fought a rising cough. She would have sworn Una had nearly harmed her if she hadn't known better. That couldn't be right. Unicorns weren't dangerous, were they?

Alexa ignored the unsettling feeling in her gut. She would go to school, talk to Mateo, and bring him to the unicorn so they could collectively decide what to do next. Together, they would find a way to save Una.

Chapter Seven

THE SUN SHONE BRIGHTLY as Alexa hurried through Riverview High School's main entrance. She grumbled and removed her sunglasses upon entering the building. After a horrible night's sleep, her eyes and head throbbed. She flexed her palms, not an easy task between the bandages and the healing cuts. She tugged the sleeves of her hoodie over her hands so no one would notice.

She glanced at her phone. Mateo had wanted to catch up with her before class, but she was running late as usual. By some miracle, she hadn't been pulled over on her way to school. One of these days, her heavy foot would turn into a speeding ticket. Once again, she texted Mateo her apologies and made her way through the teenage crowd.

As usual, everyone ignored Alexa, slipping like a determined shadow through the crowd. She belonged to none of the various social groups. Even the other weirdos didn't claim her. She and Mateo existed as an island of two. Two wacky peas in a pod.

Alexa entered her Advanced Placement Literature and Composition class right when the bell buzzed. She plopped into her assigned seat in a daze, picking at her bandaged hands. The urge to scratch had worsened between home and the drive to school.

"Everybody pull out your plays," Ms. Thurston directed from the head of the classroom. A bright-eyed, no-nonsense teacher, she thoughtfully surveyed her students. "Let's discuss last night's assignment."

Alexa retrieved the play she had struggled to read the night before: Anton Chekov's *The Seagull*. She flipped through the pages, forcing her fuzzy brain to recall what she had read between thoughts of Una. The memory of the Bright One pointing its horn at her heart left a hollow twist in Alexa's gut. The unicorn was frightened. Of course, it would be in a bad mood.

Ms. Thurston asked the class to ponder the question she scrawled on the whiteboard: "Do you identify with any of the characters in *The Seagull*, and if so, why?"

School, she needed to focus on school. Who were the main characters again? They were all so dramatic and annoying.

Several students answered, but Alexa barely heard them until the person beside her said, "Masha isn't the only one in love with someone she couldn't have."

Alexa's cheeks flared. Lost between the thoughts of Una and Chekov, she had forgotten about her wonderful and yet awful feelings for Sidhit Diyani.

Alexa glanced Sid's way, and her stomach flipped—just like it always did—every time she dared to glimpse her crush. Besides being intelligent and handsome, Sid was popular and a star player on the varsity soccer team.

Much like Masha from *The Seagull*, Alexa crushed on the unattainable. The way Sid flipped his dark hair out of his big, dark eyes made her chest contract. God, he was just so beautiful. And so absolutely perfect.

"I mean, look at all the characters." Sid waved a hand and cracked a confident grin. "No one ends up with the person they want. It's depressing."

And her unrequited adoration of Sid was also depressing. He didn't even know Alexa existed.

As class meandered along, Alexa covered the margins of her notes with unicorn shapes. While most students took notes on their tablets or laptops, Alexa liked the feeling of a pencil between her fingers, even when injured. The voices of her fellow students dulled when she pictured Una standing glorious and shining in the park, nose to the wind. The light had dazzled off its coat even when the sun hid behind a cloud.

Shading a sketch of Una's left eye, the sound of someone leaning back in their chair caught Alexa's attention. She looked up to see Sid craning his neck, grinning as he surveyed the drawings dancing across her notebook.

Alexa flinched and slapped a hand across her notes. A hundred pricks of pain attacked her bandaged palms, causing her to gasp. Startled by the gesture, Sid jumped in his seat and muffled a laugh. His quivering smile made her cheeks flush hotter than before.

Alexa ducked her head and slid deep into her seat. She pulled her knit cap farther down her brow and tried to become invisible.

"Nice deer," Sid whispered, the alluring grin still on his face.

She sunk further as breakfast threatened to make an encore performance.

"They're unicorns," Alexa managed to squeak.

"Alexa, would you like to contribute?" Ms. Thurston's bright voice broke through their hushed conversation.

Startled out of her personal drama and into the sight of twenty pairs of eyes, Alexa swallowed hard. Like most of Alexa's classes, this class comprised the overly ambitious vying for recognition. They came from families who believed in the sacred duty of intellectual rigor. When anyone stumbled, they smelled blood in the water.

"Uh ... well, I think Trigorin is the villain in this play," Alexa spoke so softly that several students leaned forward to hear her better. Ms. Thurston put a hand to her ear, signaling Alexa to speak up. "What he does to Nina is horrible, and he doesn't have to do it. He has plenty of women who want him, so why does he have to hurt Nina? He's super self-absorbed and doesn't think about anyone but himself."

Ms. Thurston's eyebrows rose, and she nodded in appreciation. "And Nina can't help but follow him. But what about Konstantin, the one who loves her? Why does she follow Trigorin instead?"

Only minutes were left in class. A chorus of bodies shifted in their seats as Ms. Thurston turned and wrote on the whiteboard. Alexa heaved a small sigh, grateful to have survived another group discussion.

"I want everyone to give me a five-hundred-word essay on why *The Seagull* is titled "*The Seagull*," Ms. Thurston said as she wrote. "The essay is due at the beginning of class on Thursday. Tonight, I want you to read the first act of *Hedda Gabbler* so we can begin to discuss it in class tomorrow."

The bell rang, and students collected their belongings. Alexa fought the desire to glance in Sid's direction as she sensed him get up from his chair. She wanted him to leave, ashamed he had caught her drawing, yet she ached to meet his eyes. God, she was so pathetic.

"Unicorns, huh?" Sid hovered next to her, a lazy grin spread across his face.

Alexa's stomach launched into a series of wicked somersaults, and she snatched up the notebook and pressed it against her chest. Her heart threatened to spill out and bleed all over her desk.

"I guess." Alexa rested her chin against the top of the notebook.

"My sister digs unicorns, too," Sid laughed. "What is it with girls and unicorns?"

Alexa's face burned as hot as the sun. She happened to know Sid's sister was twelve. "I just like the shape."

"No, but really." Sid sat on the edge of his desk. "Naija has posters of unicorns all over her bedroom walls. Are they, like, better than horses or something?"

"Well, the one in my backyard is pretty cool," Alexa said without thinking.

"The what in what?" Sid chuckled.

Alexa clapped a hand to her mouth and then squeaked as her palm cried out in pain. Most of the kids in class saw her as a weird, "artsy" girl, so what not lean into it? "I found it in the park yesterday afternoon. In the women's bathroom."

"The women's bathroom? Classic. And now it's where?"

"Our shed out back. It's being super needy, to be honest." Alexa joined him as he snickered, her laughter dancing on the edge of panic. "You should meet it. Seriously."

"Oh, yeah?" Sid shook his head as he gathered his books. "You live on Carmichael Ridge, right?"

"How did you—oh, you must know because of Andrea."

Sid was a star on the boys' soccer team, and Andrea was on the girls' team. He and her sister's social circle often overlapped. If Andrea knew how she felt about Sid, she would taunt Alexa until her dying day.

"Well, maybe I'll take you up on that." Sid walked backward down the aisle of desks. He shook his hair out of his eyes and disappeared into the hallway with a slight, tantalizing smirk.

"Oh," Alexa sighed as he left the room. She wished to follow in his wake. Hell, she would follow him anywhere if he asked.

Alexa drifted out of the classroom, notebooks still against her chest. Half her thoughts stumbled behind the boy she adored, while the others fixated on the surreal memory of Una lying behind her father's boat. She let the two ideas converge into one: Alexa introducing Una to Sid, and Sid clutching her hand, unable to believe what stood before him.

The thought stuck in her mind as she headed to her second-period class.

Chapter Eight

LUNCH PERIOD COULDN'T arrive soon enough.

Soundgarden blasted through Alexa's headphones as she headed from one side of the high school to the other. Alexa didn't spend lunch in the cafeteria, unlike the rest of her cohort. Instead, she retrieved her locally sourced organic meal from her locker and bounded up a set of back stairs to her hidden midday sanctuary—the drawing and painting studio.

Alexa said hello to the two art teachers in their shared office. They had allowed Alexa and Mateo to spend their lunches together in the art room starting in early September.

The studio was a simple, large room with beige walls covered in recent student art projects. A wall full of cabinets and shelves held an array of art supplies. Large prints of their teachers' favorite artists hung in the few open spaces. Ms. Ash was on a Van Gogh kick lately.

A slight figure nibbling on crackers and a Diet Coke sat at one of the tables.

"Hey, bestie!" Alexa smiled and waved to the most wonderful and precious person in her life, Mateo.

"About time." Mateo leaped up from his seat and gave Alexa a big hug. Even though she had seen him less than a day ago, it felt as if decades had passed. Heck, maybe even a century. Mateo still didn't know about yesterday's wild adventure. One simply couldn't explain a unicorn over text.

"You have less than five minutes to spill what happened to you yesterday," Mateo said, flicking his bleached bangs from his eyes. He wore a frayed Packers t-shirt beneath a neon zip-up hoodie. Queer positive pins covered the collar of his sweatshirt, and beaded rainbow bracelets wrapped his brown wrists.

"Of course." Alexa flopped into the chair beside him, vibrating with secrets. Mateo was the only person in the whole world she would consider sharing such an impossible thing as a unicorn from another world. However, even he wouldn't believe her until he saw Una in person.

"Can you come over to my place after school?" Alexa whispered, checking over her shoulders in case the art teachers decided to wander into the studio.

"First, you should be lucky I forgive you for completely ignoring me yesterday," Mateo grumbled as he set aside his smartphone. "BRB? You'll never believe what I found. Not cool."

"I'm so sorry, yesterday was just—wild. You'll understand when you see what *it* is."

"What is this?" Mateo grabbed one of Alexa's wrists. "What have you done to your hands?"

Alexa slipped from his grip and stuck her hands beneath the table, rubbing her itching palms against her thighs. "Nothing. I mean—you'll understand when you come over."

"Mmm, and the mystery continues. If it's another Nirvana vinyl discovery, I'm going to lose my shit."

"Oh, no, no, no ... thing like that." Alexa wanted to burst out of her skin. "This is something completely different."

Mateo frowned, studying her from head to foot. "Are you okay?"

Alexa shook her head and picked at her bandages. Making it to lunch without going nuts had felt like a minor miracle. Now, to survive the rest of the day. She picked at her lunch but had no interest in eating. Usually, her mother's leftover macaroni and cheese was her favorite.

"You've ... gotta see this thing." Alexa sipped her container of oat milk, which her mom included with every lunch. Nope, that wasn't going down well either. She tossed the cardboard container into the nearest trash can.

"Whoa, can't you just tell me?"

Alexa's left foot tapped an irregular rhythm on the classroom floor. "You won't believe me if I tell you."

"Lex ..." Mateo pressed a hand against her forehead. "Are you sick? Do I need to text your Mom? Cynthia must be worried about you, too."

"Like I said, you won't believe me if you don't see it. I put it in the back shed, behind my dad's boat."

"The shed? Seriously, just tell me what the hell is going on."

Alexa grabbed an apple from her lunch and turned it over in quivering hands. "I know, but you'll never believe it. Promise you'll come to my house after school."

"Must be something good." Mateo frowned and snatched the apple from her. He bit into the fruit and sighed. "Mmm, that's totally from a local orchard. Can your parents adopt me for a couple weeks?"

Alexa, ready to jump out of her skin, needed something to keep her hands occupied. She pulled off her stocking cap and picked at the pilled yarn on its surface. Usually, her anxiety caused her to fold into the fetal position. Una's discovery was different. She might lose her mind if Mateo didn't come over and see her secret.

"Ok, then, my favorite weirdo." Mateo watched her as she toyed with her hat, dropping one speck of yarn after another onto the floor. "I'll follow you home and see whatever this thing is. But, you're okay? I'm worried about you."

"Sure, yeah, okay." Alexa kicked at the steel legs of their art table.

"Lex, you are so totally freaked. This better be good."

Alexa giggled. "You have no idea."

Surges of panic and the sensation of losing touch with reality accompanied Alexa as she trundled through the rest of the school day. Despite her mental chaos, the comfort of routine eventually kicked in by early afternoon. She even raised her hand once in Psych class and answered one of Mrs. Andersen's questions about the difference between industrial and organizational psychology.

Finally, she reached her last class of the day, AP United States History. Settling into the back of the classroom, a new sort of anxiety arose. Una would expect Alexa and Mateo to devise a plan to save it. And what about the monster? Didn't Una say it might arrive at any second?

Mr. Hines had spent the class outlining Alexander Hamilton's significant accomplishments. There were many, and Alexa felt he was about to spend the entire class period waxing poetic about his favorite founding father. Alexa copied his notes without thinking and tried not to count the minutes until the end of the day.

"Draw any new unicorn pictures?"

Alexa jumped in her seat.

Sid.

Much like AP Lit, AP US History had assigned seats arranged alphabetically. This arraignment meant Sid had sat near her during the past decade of classes together. Both a joy and a curse once they hit puberty.

Alexa wiggled in her seat. "Um, no?"

"So, does your invitation stand?"

Alexa's heart pounded in an unwieldy rhythm. "Invitation?"

"To see your unicorn?" Laughter danced in his eyes.

He must be making a joke. She could too. "Sure, why not?"

"What time?"

"Mr. Dayani, please focus," Mr. Hines said with a subtle shift in his monotonous tone.

Sid flashed his teacher a guilty grin. "Sorry, Mr. Hines."

The bell rang, and Alexa scrambled out of her seat. Tucking her thick history textbook into her stuffed backpack, she tried avoiding further engagement with Sid. Sid, however, had other ideas.

"What happened to your hands?"

"I fell." Alexa flexed her fingers and drew them behind her back. The scratches on her fingers had become progressively angrier after a day of holding pencils and opening doors. The gauze and tape were puckered and frayed. Alexa struggled to ignore the discomfort. She rubbed her right palm against her jeans and prayed to the gods of hydrocortisone.

"Must have been some fall. So, what time am I stopping by?"

Alexa barked out a laugh. "Four?"

"Great. See you then."

Speechless, Alexa refused to stare when Sid loped over to his group of friends at the classroom door. Two whole conversations in one day. That had never happened before. Her hands shook as she tossed everything in her backpack. A smile threatened to stretch across her face.

Throats cleared from the doorway. Sid's friends, Drew and Travon, stared in her direction. Mocking grins distorted their handsome faces. The two boys didn't feel the need to lower their voices when they asked why the hell Sid had talked to Courtney Love. A part of Alexa's chest cracked, aware of the nickname many of her classmates used.

Alexa deflated, sat back down, and pretended to take additional notes from the whiteboard. The posse of toxic masculinity needed to go before she could gather the courage to leave. As if on cue, they burst into a chorus of sardonic laughter, their cruelty following them down the hallway.

Tears pricked Alexa's eyes. The injury of their disdain ran deep. At least school was over. She had survived another day.

Pulling out her phone, Alexa typed, *I'm heading out to the parking lot in five minutes.*

Pulsing ellipses appeared immediately, and Mateo replied, *About time. Let's go see your big surprise.*

Chapter Nine

ALEXA LOST THE ABILITY to speak when she parked in her family's looping driveway. Mateo prattled on as usual, talking about the latest social media drama while they traipsed along the flagstone path that ran from her front yard to the back. Soon, Una wasn't going to be only her secret to bear. She anticipated Mateo's potential freakout, and a smile curved her lips.

They walked through the side gate into the backyard. The afternoon had taken a dreary turn. The sky had darkened to a slate gray, and thunder rolled far in the distance.

As they approached the shed, Alexa noticed that the once-green lawn surrounding it had withered and died sometime while she was gone. The verdant Kentucky bluegrass had completely dried out, and several patches appeared to be rotting. An unpleasant smell radiated from the rotting parts.

"Did something die nearby?" Mateo waved a hand under his nose. "Cuz that's foul."

"No idea." The grass's dead zone crept out in finger-like tendrils from the shed's foundation. Mateo poked a foot at one particularly stinky patch. The turf crunched beneath his feet.

"Yuck." Mateo stuck out his tongue in disgust. "Is this what you wanted to show me? I hope not."

Where have you been, Alexa Baxter? You said you would not be gone for too long. The Bright One's bizarre voice rang through her head.

Alexa flinched. She had forgotten the unnatural sound of Una's voice. Alexa turned to Mateo. Did he hear the unicorn, too? Mateo continued to prod the dried grass with a deepening grimace.

"Huh," Alexa said.

"Huh, what?"

"Did you hear anything?"

"Like what?"

"Like, uh, voice or something?"

"A voice? Other than yours?"

"Yeah. Like a voice you can only hear in your head."

"Oh, Lex. Are you hearing voices? Did you stay up too late reading all weekend? I know sometimes when you're not sleeping enough—"

"No, not—ugh, okay." Alexa raised her arms to center herself. The sound of something falling echoed within the shed.

Did you not hear me the first time, Alexa Baxter? I am not exaggerating. I need to know if it is safe for me to come out. I can hear someone else with you. What is going on?

Alexa held her breath, waiting one more time for Mateo to react.

Mateo placed his hands on his hips and narrowed his eyes. "Alexa, I'm worried about you. I need you to tell me about the voices you're hearing. What are they saying? Maybe you just need to lie down. You're all jerky like when you drink a quad too fast."

Another bang tumbled through the shed.

Mateo twitched in surprise. "What was that?"

"You heard that, right?" Alexa grasped her friend's hand.

"Ugh, yeah. Did you, like, rescue a cat or a dog or something? Is that what all this is about?"

"Well, I sort of rescued something." Alexa led Mateo toward the shed, avoiding the especially rancid bits of grass.

Nearly eight hours had passed since she last looked upon the unicorn. A shiver quivered down her spine as she turned the shed's doorknob. She jerked open the door and stepped into the gloom. The shape of Una was visible despite the dark interior. Silver light limned its graceful form as the unicorn slipped out from behind the boat.

Finally, you have returned. We need to talk, Alexa Baxter.

Alexa turned to Mateo; voice hushed in reverence. "Are you ready?"

"Hon, ready for what?"

Alexa switched on the lights. Una snorted and pricked its ears forward, eyes blinking rapidly from the sudden flood of illumination.

I have waited all day for you to return. And now I am hungry. I require solid food. Una stomped a hoof and blew out another sharp snort. The unicorn tossed its head in annoyance and smacked its tail against a bag of lawn fertilizer.

Mateo's eyes bulged. His jaw dropped. He tried to speak, but words failed him. He wavered on his feet, and Alexa lifted an arm to steady him.

"Lex," he whispered, "is that?"

"Yeah, it is."

"Oh … I … whoa. Girl, I can't … whoa."

"Right?"

"Holy shit, Lex."

"I know."

Is this the one you talked about earlier? The unicorn cocked its and studied Alexa's best friend. Mateo said nothing, continuing to grip Alexa's arm for dear life. *Is he broken? What is wrong with this Earth creature?*

"Well, unicorns don't exist here. Remember my reaction when I first saw you?" Alexa gave Mateo a nudge as his eyes glazed over.

Need I remind you that I am not a unicorn. Una's tail whipped with irritation. *I am a Bright One. Please do not confuse your friend by misnaming me in your presence.*

"Yeah, sorry, Una."

Mateo held up a hand, eyes still wide. "Wait, are you *talking* to it?"

"Yeah. You can't hear, Una? I wonder why I can."

"Uh, no!" Mateo snapped, throwing his arms in a frantic arc. "What are you hearing? It's not making any noise. Except for snorts, I guess. Do you somehow understand unicorn snorting language?"

Alexa shook her head. "For me, it's like Una is speaking to me telepathically. I hear it, but not in my ears, just in my head. Super weird, right? Oh, sorry, I should introduce you to each other. Una, this is Mateo. Mateo, this is Una."

I mean, no offense. I expected someone a little more ... composed. And he speaks with too much volume. Una flattened its ears.

"I think he's taking your introduction well." Alexa shrugged.

"I think I need some air," Mateo gasped, leaning against her. "This is ... too much. This can't be happening."

I agree. I cannot take another moment in this dusty, dirty building. Una shook itself, mane flying and light refracting off its horn.

"I should probably cover you up again before you go outside," Alexa said.

I have reached the end of my patience. Please get out of my way. The unicorn lowered its head and pointed its horn toward the door.

"Just wait a second. No one should be home for a while. It's Tuesday, Mom has Pilates, and Andrea has volleyball practice. Dinner's at seven, so Dad won't be home until then, either." The unicorn was clearly cranky from being cooped up all day. A decent meal might be the trick. "I may as well let you in the house. We need to find something you'll eat. Mom should have plenty of leftovers in the fridge."

Mateo woke from his haze of disbelief. "You're going to let it in the house? You can't be serious. What if the unicorn, like, breaks something?"

"Why not? Una's not that big."

"OMG, this is just too weird." Mateo ran his fingers through his hair. "How is this possible? How the hell do you have a unicorn in your parent's shed?"

"I found Una in the park yesterday. It was trapped in the women's bathroom, so I helped free it. That's how I got these." Alexa raised her bandaged hands. "Watch out, that horn is sharper than it looks."

"This is insane." Mateo backed closer to the still-open door. "Isn't there someone you should call?"

"Like who?"

"Animal control? Or maybe a wildlife rehab center?"

"Mateo, you're joking. Wildlife rehab? This unicorn isn't a wild animal. It's an alien creature from another world."

Mateo coughed. "Did you say *alien?*"

Alexa Baxter! I require sustenance. And then, we will discuss what to do next. Una, having lost patience, leaped over the wheel of a bicycle in its path. Mateo and Alexa ran into eachother to give the unicorn some room. Una shoved them with its shoulder and trotted into the backyard.

"Una, wait. Maybe you shouldn't—"

Alexa and Mateo scrambled out of the shed behind the unicorn.

Despite the overcast skies, Una sparkled as it jogged a loop around Alexa's backyard. Swishing its tale, Una easily navigated the steps up to the back deck abutting their kitchen.

"This is insane," Mateo repeated and followed the unicorn. "What are you going to do with it? Her? Him? They?"

"'It,' I think? I haven't asked Una's preferred pronouns." Alexa also hurried after the unicorn. "I was hoping you could help me figure out what to do."

Please hurry, Alexa Baxter. Una stood at the sliding glass doors and appreciated its reflection in the window while waiting for Alexa and Mateo to catch up. The unicorn blinked its long, golden lashes, cocked its head, then blew on the window pane.

Alexa unlocked and slid the door open. The unicorn took several deep sniffs before walking into the kitchen. Una's cloven hooves clicked across the tiled floor. Alexa was grateful her mother had redesigned the kitchen several years ago for better "workflow." Una easily navigated the kitchen table, island, and wrap-around counters. The high ceiling and recessed lighting allowed the unicorn to stand upright without poking its horn in unwanted places.

Is this where you prepare food? Una wandered around the central island counter and sniffed at the sink. The unicorn pressed its muzzle against the polished granite countertop, fogging the surface with its breath.

"Yep. Spectacular, right? Mom's kitchen was featured in a local interior design magazine a year ago. Let's see if I can find something in the fridge. Mom always has tons of random stuff." Alexa approached her mother's oversized stainless-steel beast of a refrigerator and opened the door. Inside was packed with fruits, vegetables, leftovers, homemade juices, nut milk, and every condiment known to man.

"Unfortunately, we don't have any meat since Mom is on a vegan-vegetarian kick. Do you eat meat?"

Do you mean the flesh of other animals?

"Yeah."

Absolutely not. Only primitive savages slaughter living creatures for food.

"Well, then, you've come to the right house."

Mateo settled upon one of the bar stools surrounding the central island. As he watched the unicorn survey the fridge interior, his mouth fell further and further open. Like her, he would need time to process the impossible creature in her kitchen. Alexa picked a variety of containers from the shelves and pulled out a long glass container of macaroni and cheese.

"So, we have stuff like apples and carrots, or what about grains? Horses eat grains, right?" She pulled a handful of spoons from the cutlery drawer and dumped them on the counter. "Let's start with ... quinoa."

Una's nostrils flared as it sniffed the spoonful. The unicorn opened its mouth, revealing pearly teeth and bizarre blue tongue. Alexa dumped the spoon's contents, and the unicorn chewed thoughtfully.

Bland. What else do you have?

"So, Alexa, you said something about Una being an alien? What did you mean by that?"

"Honestly, we haven't talked many details." Alexa opened another glass container. "This is basmati rice." She dropped another spoonful into the unicorn's mouth.

It is better than the first, but not by much.

"We'll keep looking," Alexa said. "So, I meant to ask you more about your origins. And what about this 'monster'? What is it? Why does it want to hurt you?"

Due to complex intergalactic and multidimensional politics, of course. They will destroy me no matter what it takes. The unicorn nodded as it chewed a spoonful of Alexa's mother's beloved baked mac-and-cheese, one of the few dishes she still used real cheese to make. *This is quite lovely. What is it?*

"You like macaroni and cheese?" Alexa laughed with a surge of relief. "How much do you want? Do you want it warmed up or like it this way?"

This temperature is sufficient. Can I eat it all?

"Sure, why not? Well, that was easy." Alexa placed the container on the floor "Everybody likes mac-and-cheese, right?"

Una shoved its nose into the dish and grunted in satisfaction.

"Alexa. I need you to focus." Mateo snapped his fingers. "You said something about monsters. What are you talking about?"

"Right. Sorry. So, how worried do we have to be about this monster showing up?"

I calculate that the monster has a considerable chance of catching up with me because I have been here for so long. The unicorn raised its head from the dish, pasta, and cheese sticking to its pink muzzle. *We must leave the moment I finish my meal. The monster will not hesitate to harm you, too.*

"But, I thought you said the monster wouldn't even notice me." The blood drained from Alexa's face. "Did you lie to me?"

Mateo leaned forward. "Lex! What did it say?"

"Una?" Alexa nudged the container of pasta with her toe to get the unicorn's attention. "Tell me the truth."

Una blinked its dazzling blue eyes. *Would you have helped me if I told you the truth?*

"Of course, I would."

I cannot count on the kindness of strangers. It is hard to trust anyone in the vast multiverse, especially after the things I have seen, heard, and run from. I was afraid you would leave me stranded on this savage planet with no one to help me. I must apologize. I am sorry. I have underestimated your kindness.

"Thanks?" Alexa frowned. "Well, Mateo. Turns out we might have to worry about a monster after all."

This meal has brought me some clarity. I believe I know what we must do next. Una lapped at the remains of its dinner. *We go west. I am unsure why, but I feel this powerful pull to go west—a feeling that helped lead me to the doorway to Earth. There must be a Rift that can take me to the next world. I have heard Earth is full of them, most placed illegally.*

"Rift?" Alexa squeaked. "What's that?"

Simple. A manufactured tear into the space-time of the multiverse. How else would we move across the lightyears?

Mateo quivered in his seat. "God, I hate the fact that—whatever—Lex, what's Una saying?"

"We have to find a door. A Rift." Alexa blinked and swallowed down the new information. Her known reality continued to unwind. If monsters and unicorns existed, why not doors to other worlds? "Can you get there on your own?" Alexa asked Una.

I need your help, Alexa Baxter. I cannot move fast enough on foot, and I do not know the ways of Earth. I do know that I do not belong here. Nor does the monster. We must go now, quickly.

"I can't just leave." Alexa grabbed the casserole container from the floor and set it in the sink. She poured warm water into the Pyrex and said, "I have school. And my parents would never let me.

"Alexa, I can't hear what Una's saying. What the hell are you two talking about?"

The deep bong of the doorbell rang through the house. Alexa and Mateo stared at each other, frozen in place. The unicorn flicked its ears and raised its head. A loud knock banged from the front door.

"Are you expecting anyone?" Mateo asked.

"No?"

What was that odd noise, Alexa Baxter?

The doorbell rang again.

"What should we do?" Alexa whispered.

"Go see who it is." Mateo slid around the island and stood next to Una. "If I need to sneak out the unicorn, please yell ... uh ... 'Mateo, let out the dog.'"

"Great idea."

For the last time, small Earth creature, I am not a unicorn. I am a Bright One. And what is a dog?

"Okay, fine, whatever." Alexa hurried out of the kitchen and toward the front door.

Her socks skidded along the polished wood floor as she turned a corner, nearly falling into a vase filled with dogwood branches. A tall figure stood on the other side of the frosted, cut-glass of their front door. She took a deep breath and opened the door to reveal Sid standing on her front porch.

"You said four o'clock, right?"

Chapter Ten

ALEXA GAPED AT THE boy who had unintentionally stolen her heart at some point during sophomore year. Words moved in a slurry from her brain, unable to process the fact that Sid stood at her front door. Looking at her. Waiting for her to speak.

His familiar Subaru Impreza was parked behind her Civic, the license plate simply reading: SID. Of course, she knew which car he drove. She had tracked its progress across the school parking lot dozens of times before and now that car was in her driveway.

She stared at him, her pulse banging wildly in her ears.

Sid raised his eyebrows. "You said, four o'clock? Am I late? Early?"

"Oh," Alexa gasped, the sound bursting out in a too-loud rush.

"Can I at least come in?" Sid shook his hair out of his eyes and Alexa died a little.

"Come in?" Unsure what to do with her hands Alexa clasped them before her, then, behind and finally dropped them to her side.

"So where do you keep the unicorn? You said something about the backyard?" He leaned forward as if part of a conspiracy. Thick lashes rimmed his beautiful dark eyes. He smelled of peppermint and citrus.

"I left it in the kitchen?" Alexa fought the urge to deeply inhale his scent.

Sid tossed his head back as he laughed. "Alexa, have I ever told you you're one of a kind? So, can I come in? It's a little chilly out here."

"Of course." Alexa stepped back to let Sid cross the WELCOME mat and enter the foyer.

"Ugh, do you need me to let the dog out?" Mateo called from the kitchen. Alexa could hear the sound of his footsteps walking down the hall. He peaked his head around the corner and his eyes widened. "Sid? Hi, uh, Sidhit—er—Sid. So, whatcha' doing here?"

"Alexa invited me to come by and see the unicorn in her backyard." Sid unzipped his letter jacket and tossed it onto the bench in the entryway. He took in the large foyer, wooden staircase, and Restoration Hardware chandelier above them. "Nice place."

"Thanks?" Alexa tugged her stocking cap lower on her head, tempted to pull it all the way over her flushed face.

"You told him about the unicorn?" Mateo glared at Alexa for a moment, then dropped his shoulders and rolled his eyes.

Mateo knew all about Alexa's long-standing crush on Sid. He had long ago diagnosed her as a hopeless romantic. Alexa agreed.

"I sure did!" Alexa's voice grew shrill as a dog's squeaky toy.

"What a freakin' day." Mateo crossed his arms over his chest and leaned his head against the wall. Sid glanced between Mateo and Alexa. Alexa shrugged and suppressed a giggle.

Una's silent voice called from the kitchen, *Do I hear another Earth creature, Alexa Baxter? You did not mention anyone else coming? Is this the one who can help us?*

"So, can I meet it?" Sid popped a thumb toward the back of Alexa's house, an uncertain grin on his lips.

Alexa straightened her shoulders. "Yes, why not? Follow me."

"No!" Mateo yelped. "Are you insane?"

"Yes, yes I am." Alexa held out a bandaged hand to Sid. "I'll show you."

Sid's hand was warm and large in hers, causing the persistent ache to settle for the first time that day. The sensation sent a thrill up her arm. She tugged him behind her and led him into the kitchen. They found Una attempting to open the refrigerator door with its teeth.

Seeing the new guest, Una let go of the door handle and pricked its ears toward Sid. *Who is this, Alexa Baxter? He is much larger than Mateo. I like his hair.*

"So do I," Alexa said. "Sid, this is Una. Una, this is Sid. A boy I know from school."

Sid's once smiling face went blank and he froze in place. He blinked wide eyes then squinted as if he didn't trust what his eyes saw. Una took several tentative steps in Sid's direction, nostrils flaring as the unicorn took in his scent. *He smells nice.*

"He sure does." Alexa couldn't want to see what happened next.

Sid put out his hand and Una brushed its muzzle against his fingers. Sid startled at the unicorn's touch.

Mateo stopped beside Alexa; his frown deeper than before. "Why would you tell him? Of all people, Lex?"

Alexa giggled, "I didn't think he'd believe me."

Una let out a grunt of approval. *I believe this one can help us. However, he is making some rather odd expressions. I believe this is not the normal way Earth creatures greet each other?*

"He's just in shock." Alexa monitored Sid's response as he stumbled over to their Pottery Barn dining set and sat in one of the six chairs. He first peered into his open hands as if touching the unicorn had answered some sort of question. Then Sid rubbed his eyes furiously before looking at Una one more time.

"Now that Sid's here, can we get back to business?" Mateo rounded on Una and Alexa.

Alexa recognized the determined set to his jaw. "Time to make a plan."

Mateo nodded. "What's the unicorn doing here, what is all this talk about monsters, and what are we going to do?"

"Exactly. Una, tell me again about that Rift-thingy."

Yes, there is another one somewhere out west. And we should head in that direction immediately. The unicorn nodded its head toward the sliding glass doors. *Shall we take your vehicle? I seem to fit in it well enough. Or do one of these others have a larger one?*

Alexa shrugged. "I'm a better driver than Mateo. We should probably take my car."

Una sighed. *Well, I sort of fit in your backseat.*

"Car?" Mateo shrilled. "Where are we going?"

Alexa waved in a westerly direction. "West?"

"This is insane." Mateo muttered, pacing the length of the kitchen.

"Wait, is the unicorn speaking to you?" Sid rose from his stupor and pointed to Una. "How's that happening?" He turned to Mateo. "Can you hear it?"

Mateo said, "Only Alexa can hear Una for some reason we have yet to understand."

"Oh, wow. Weird." Sid ran his hands over his face. "This is so fucking unreal."

This is not the time to discuss means of communication. We have more important issues at hand. When are we leaving?

"Soon, I think," Alexa said.

"Where are you from, Una?" Mateo said, impatience coloring his voice.

None of your business small, loud Earth creature. All I need from your lot is to get me as far away from the monster and to a Rift as quickly as possible. The monster will do the most horrible things to me—to us. You have no idea of the terror that follows me across worlds.

"Una's more worried about the monster right now," Alexa translated. "And I am too. We have no idea what's after Una."

Sid sat up in his chair. "Wait, did you say *monster*?"

The monster is a cruel, evil. Without remorse. They have been sent to hunt my people into extinction. There are so few of us left. I refused to give up and accept oblivion. I will not stop running as long and far as necessary.

Alexa translated. Mateo blanched. Sid winced.

"You're not kidding, are you?" Sid turned to Alexa. "Real monsters?"

And this is why we most go, Alexa Baxter. Now. I can feel the pull, the path to escape calls me. This feeling must be a sign I can find refuge beyond that door. Perhaps a place where I can find my people again. Or a safe world. Time is running out. We must go.

"Just, hold on one more minute." Alexa raised her hands as the unicorn tossed its head. "We can't just up and take off. It's not that simple. We're not the adults here. Well, barely adults. If we take off, our parents are going to flip out."

"Take off?" Mateo wrung his hands. "What do you mean, take off? I have an exam tomorrow in English class."

"This is unbelievable." Sid covered his face with his hands. "I should have gone to McDonald's with Travon. I could still go, right? Should I go?"

Ignoring Sid, Alexa explained, "I know, I told Una we can't just get in my car and drive west. My parents would freak out. How do I explain Una to my mom?"

"Yeah, I think I should go." Sid stood up, wobbling on his feet. For a moment, Alexa thought he might tip over until Sid returned to his seat. "Nope, guess I'm not moving. Ugh, I think I might puke."

"You're absolutely right, Lex." Mateo said. "We can't just leave town without trying to explain what's happening to our family first."

This is intolerable. Alexa, we must go right this very second. There is something gathering near us. I have felt this before. The monster will be here any moment.

"Hey, where's the nearest bathroom?" Sid let out a watery burp.

The cacophony of voices spun around Alexa. Distant thunder punctuated the chaos. Mateo engaged in a one-sided argument with Una, while the unicorn waved its horn in increasingly violent gestures. Sid dry-heaved and clapped his hands over his mouth. He rose in a rush, hurried to the sink, and let loose the contents of his stomach. The thick, wet gagging sound and the splash of vomit caused Alexa's stomach to turn too. Mateo and Una moaned in a chorus of disgust.

A second volley of thunder rumbled closer than the first. The unicorn flinched and turned toward the kitchen's sliding doors. The sky had grown darker since Sid arrived. Alexa went to Una's side as a mountainous thunderhead expanded across the sky above her house. Viens of acid green lighting burst against the roiling clouds. A dark finger of cloud began to descend into Alexa's yard at an unnatural speed.

Una let out a small cry and knocked against Alexa. *We are too late. The monster is here.*

Day became night. Several more winding tendrils joined the first. The vaporous branches reached for the back shed, filling the air. When thunder crashed again it sounded more like a roar than an act of nature.

The cloud was alive and searching for Una.

Mateo, whimpering at Alexa's side, pressed his hands against the window glass as the cloud monster gathered its fingers around the shed door. With a sharp crack of breaking wood, the door was hurled through the yard like a flimsy piece of paper.

"Shit, are you seeing this?" Sid joined them, wiping his mouth with the back of his sleeve.

Another roar bellowed from the heavens.

Run! We must run now!

Alexa turned to the two boys and the unicorn. "Get in my car."

Chapter Eleven

THE HOUSE SHUDDERED on its foundation as another roar erupted from the sky. Each teenager screamed at a different pitch and raced through the front door. Bodies collided in their desperate attempt to escape.

Alexa slammed the front door behind Una as the unicorn scrabbled out, heading for Alexa's Civic. A behemoth of black cloud rose above the roofline from the back of her house. Lightning surged and crackled in the thickest parts of the living storm. A dreadful rumble shook the earth beneath her.

Alexa fingered her key fob, opening the locks on her car. Sid and Mateo threw open both of the back passenger doors. The unicorn shouldered its way past Mateo and scrambled into the backseat.

Mateo threw his hands in the air and shrieked, "I got shotgun!"

Another explosion tore across the sky. Alexa tripped and fell to her knees. She crawled to the driver's side and grabbed the door handle. A shadow brushed against her back, plucking at the tender place in her skull Una had probed the day before.

Ragged claws scraped across her brain as Alexa cried, "Let go of me!"

She threw open the door, snapped on her seatbelt, and slammed her door, cutting off the cloud-fingers. The talons continued to reach for her, scraping against her window. Alexa's half-dozen keys turned into a thousand as she tried to find the right one.

"Oh God, oh God, oh God," Mateo sobbed, curling into the passenger seat.

"What do I do?" Sid shook his hands at the unicorn taking up most of the backseat.

"Push your way in!" Alexa shouted. "Una, you have to make room for him."

Alexa found the correct key and slammed it into the ignition. Sid heaved himself into the backseat while Una's legs went in every direction to make room. Their bodies tangled into a hopeless jumble.

Damn your big feet, Earth creature, Una silently bellowed in Sid's ear.

"Just go, Alexa. Go!" Mateo pounded the dashboard.

The engine revved—crap, she had it in neutral. The Smashing Pumpkins thrashed their guitars over the speakers before the drums came barreling after. Alexa shifted into reverse and slammed her foot against the accelerator. The sky descended to the earth, smashing into the empty air where the Civic sat moments before.

Alexa wrapped her fingers around the steering wheel, shifted into drive, and sent the car barreling down the street. Instead of heading for one of the main roads full of rush hour traffic, she sped deeper into her neighborhood, a sudden, crazy plan taking shape. They skidded around the first turn, wheels protesting. Una's horn slashed the air inches from her face.

"Sid, you've gotta keep Una's horn under control!" Alexa cried.

A flash of lightning sliced across the car's hood. Alexa jerked in her seat but kept her hands steady on the wheel. Her hands protested. She ignored the pain, letting adrenaline fuel her every move. Alexa loved to drive, and this was her element. She lacked confidence in many parts of her life but felt exhilaration behind the wheel.

The thunder faded behind them, and the unnatural clouds thinned. The monster had driven them deeper into her otherwise quiet neighborhood. If she didn't think fast, the monster would trap them in one of the many cul-de-sacs or dead ends.

"Lex, we're going the wrong way," Mateo whimpered, braced against the passenger door.

"No, I have a plan. I know where to take us." Driving at least twenty miles over the speed limit, Alexa noticed a middle-aged woman shouting at them from her front porch.

"Doesn't she see the monster?" Sid shoved one of Una's legs off his lap as they passed the angry neighbor.

The monster reveals itself only to those they hunt. Una twisted in the backseat. *Stupid Earth creature, you are sitting on my tail.*

Sid sputtered as Una's front hooves braced against his chest. "I shoulda gone to McDonalds."

Alexa glanced in her rearview mirror. The monster hadn't stopped its pursuit. She could better see the monster's sheer size as the trees around them thinned. The clouds covered the western horizon.

"Oh God, oh God, oh God," Mateo chanted. His knuckles had turned white from gripping the seat too hard.

Alexa Baxter, we need to move faster. So much faster.

"I know, I know," Alexa said as she sped the car toward the rounded end of a cul-de-sac. They were running out of road, but Alexa knew the neighborhood in and out, especially before she had a car and was stuck riding her bicycle everywhere. "Hang on to something!"

A bike path cleaved between two towering McMansions along one edge of the cul-de-sac. She prayed that no one felt like an afternoon ride and shot the Honda down the narrow gravel path. Her Civic clipped the curb, ripping a tear through the sod of a once pristine frown lawn. Mateo screamed.

The bike path ran parallel to a playground occupied by two kids on a swing set. They jumped off their swings and stared in delighted horror as Alexa's car descended the bike path.

"Turning sharp right," Alexa hollered and barreled across the basketball court.

A parking lot lay on the other side of the playground, and the lot exited onto a county highway, which would leave them straight toward the interstate. If they reached I-94, they might make it out of Riverview alive. Alexa tightened her grip on the steering wheel and directed her car that way.

Alexa's satellite radio changed songs. Veruca Salt's drummer tapped out several dashing notes on the high hat before the guitars dropped into a banger of a song. The music rushed over her senses, sending a fresh surge of manic courage through her limbs.

Dodging a set of monkey bars and spring riders, wheels ripping up the earth, three teenagers and one grumpy unicorn sailed across the park. To their left, a softball game paused mid-inning. Players and crowd alike gaped as the Honda raced behind the stands. A girl in pigtails clapped in delight.

Behind them, the cloud monster had slackened in size, falling further behind. They might get away after all. Alexa continued to ride the waves of adrenaline signing through her body. Never had she experienced such clarity, such impenetrable focus as she drove through a stop sign and turned onto the county highway. The interstate was only a few miles away.

"Are we gonna make it?" Mateo stared out the rear window at the receding monster.

"Damn right, we are." Alexa laughed and slammed her foot on the gas.

"Holy shit, Alexa, you really know how to drive," Sid shouted over the loud music. He and Una had nearly sorted out their positions in the backseat.

Mateo turned back to Sid. "Yeah, her driving instructor said he'd never seen anyone so—*Alexa!*"

An enormous white truck nearly side-swiped them. The driver blasted his horn and raised a defiant middle finger in their direction. A round of relieved curses murmured through the Civic.

I have underestimated you, Alexa Baxter. You move this vehicle with excellent skill. The way is clear. Now, get us out of here. Una squirmed in the backseat while smacking Sid repeatedly in the face with its tail.

Alexa turned to the on-ramp, sweeping past another red stoplight. More horns sounded in their wake. The monster continued to diminish against the horizon.

The afternoon traffic flowed in a steady stream toward the Twin Cities. Most commuters headed in the opposite direction as people returned from a long day in the Cities. Traffic ought to be relatively light until they reached St. Paul.

Alexa slowed to the speed of the surrounding traffic. They had been lucky to get out of Riverview without a cop on their tails—time to be smart and stay off the highway patrol's radar. Her heart slowed, falling into a more regular rhythm.

They had left in such a hurry that there was no time to think. Alexa patted her left and then right pocket. She didn't have her phone. She usually sensed its absence right away, like missing a limb. Well, shit.

Sid and the unicorn finally sorted out their backseat arrangement. Una emitted a string of curses Alexa had heard a few times before. The unicorn's alien swear words were violent and guttural.

"Una, just stay calm. Sid's trying to help." Alexa said and, in the same breath, hissed, "I can't believe I forgot my phone. Dammit."

"You forgot your phone?" Mateo said as he held up his smartphone.

"Yeah, probably on the counter somewhere." Alexa's adrenaline rush faded, and the reality of the situation came into focus.

An SUV passed their left side. The pale moon of a child's face pressed against his window. His eyes rounded, and he pointed a chubby finger at the unicorn. Una couldn't stay out in the open.

Alexa said, "Guys, take the blanket back there and cover Una. People are starting to notice."

"Yeah, hang on." Sid raised his arms as Una wiggled onto his lap. "Dude, you have to stop doing that, or I won't be able to cover you."

You are causing significant pain in my back. I am simply trying to find a comfortable position. Una continued to grunt, butting its haunches against Sid's window while the unicorn's tail lashed against Alexa's back seat.

A hoof knocked against Alexa's headrest. "Careful. Both of you."

There is not enough room in this seat. Una's horn swung dangerously near Mateo's face.

"Whoa, chill, Una. I don't want to lose an eye." Mateo grabbed a loose side of the blanket and haphazardly tossed it over Una's flanks.

Una gave one more heave and twisted its body in the opposite direction as Sid and Mateo carefully covered the unicorn's blazing coat. The unicorn grimaced and laid its head in Sid's lap, its sapphire eyes burning with something akin to hatred. The Bright One mostly disappeared beneath a layer of plaid, and each Earthling in the car let out a relieved sigh.

Alexa sank into her seat. They did it. They had outrun a giant-ass monster. Driving across the St. Croix River, Alexa could see what was left of the alien clouds disappear behind the rise of the river bluffs.

Chapter Twelve

"HOLY CRAP, IS EVERYONE okay?" Alexa looked at the three sets of frightened faces in her car.

Mateo and Sid nodded. Una grunted and settled further into the backseat, muttering unpleasantries about stupid Earth creatures.

They continued steadily along I-94 west, slipping through the bustling suburbs ringing the Twin Cities. Darkness fell as late afternoon shifted towards night. Alexa turned on her headlights and focused on staying just a little over the speed limit.

Una directed Alexa to continue heading west but on a more southerly route. As the feeling of exhilaration sloughed from her senses, a bone-deep ache settled into her hands. She turned her left one over. Blood seeped through the gaps in her strained bandages.

"So, where exactly are we going?" Sid made one last attempt to readjust the blanket over Una.

I need to be able to breathe. Una shook the blanket off its head. The unicorn's horn glowed like a beacon even in the failing sunlight.

Sid clenched his fists, a series of emotions crossing his face. "But, seriously. Where are we heading? When can we go home?"

"I don't know ... Una?" Alexa's throat tightened at the mention of home. She had a feeling they weren't going home anytime soon. They couldn't stop yet or even consider turning around.

Mateo had a driver's license, just like Alexa and Sid, but if she was honest, the fact that he ever passed his driver's test was a minor miracle. He drove like an old man, avoided the interstate at all costs, and was sloppy with his breaks. What sort of driver was Sid? Alexa studied him in the rearview mirror. He sat in a daze, his eyes occasionally straying to the unicorn's horn and its head in his lap.

We keep going west.

"We keep going west?" Alexa said. "And how far?"

I cannot say, Alexa Baxter. But, I sense we shall travel a great distance.

"Great." Alexa slouched, the weight of the world settling upon her shoulders. After sleeping poorly the night before, exhaustion hung behind her eyes. How far was a great distance? South Dakota? Nebraska? Colorado? Or further than that?

"Lex, how far?" Mateo poked her shoulder.

"A great distance," Alexa said and fought back a yawn.

"What does that mean?"

"Hell, if I know."

"Maybe we should just dump the unicorn and go home?" Sid muttered. The unicorn squirmed. "I'm just kidding, dude!"

You are greatly mistaken if you think the monster will not come after you, too. Now that they know you are helping me, they will follow all of us to the ends of the earth unless I get out here first.

"We're not dumping Una," Mateo said despite missing Una's threats. "We can't abandon it now, not after what we just witnessed."

"And the monster would come after us anyway," Alexa said. "I agree with Mateo. We can't leave Una to face that horrible thing."

"Then, let's regroup." Mateo held up his phone. "I've got my phone, but Alexa doesn't have hers. Luckily, I keep a charger in her car, so my phone is set. Sid, you've got yours?"

Sid also raised his smartphone. "Yeah, got it."

"Great," Mateo said. "Ok, next issue—money. Does anyone have any cash on them?"

Alexa shook her head. "I only have my keys, car, and the clothes on my back. Oh God, my mom is gonna flip."

"Yep, mine too." Mateo scanned his phone. He was smart enough to have a pocket attached to the back of his phone that held his ID and check card. "I have my card. Sid?"

"I've got sixty in cash," Sid replied. He attempted to rest his hands next to the unicorn's head, but Una shook him off. "I don't think the unicorn likes me very much."

How many times must I repeat myself? I am not a unicorn. I am a Bright One.

"Una, please be chill." Alexa rolled her shoulders to loosen the tension in her back. "I mean, I just saved you from a monster, and I'm super chill."

I do not understand. Why would you want me to be cold?

"I have enough in checking to keep us afloat for a few days," Mateo said. "But you're gonna have to pay me back for this."

"Always do," Alexa said.

"Yeah, you got it." Sid rested his hands behind his head since Una wouldn't let him touch it.

"Next, we need to come up with a story for our parents," Mateo said. "I'll say I'm staying at Alexa's for dinner tonight, so I'll head my mom off for a little while. Sid, what about you?"

"Shit, I completely forgot, I was supposed to pick up my sister from ballet class." Sid checked his phone. "Ten minutes ago. Ugh, I have to call my parents. They're going to be so pissed."

"Text them that you had to help a friend at the last minute," Mateo directed. "We need more time to figure out our stories."

"I'm going to be grounded until college," Sid grumbled as he typed in the excuse that would set the next round of chaos into motion.

"Great. That's a start, right?" Alexa said. "See, Una, I told you he'd figure out what to do."

Una snorted and said nothing.

Alexa ignored the unicorn's silence. "I think I can handle another hour of driving. Then I need to take a break. Sid, can you take over?"

"Sure, but I have no idea where we're going."

Alexa tried to meet the unicorn's eyes in the rearview mirror. "How long are we staying on this road?"

Until we reach the following interstate heading west.

"Can you be more specific?" Alexa said.

I am a stranger in this world, Alexa Baxter. I can sense when we have to change roads, but that is all I know.

"Una isn't sure how far we're going," Alexa said. "But we got this, right? All three of us can take turns. And I'll tell you when Una wants us to merge onto a different road."

"How very positive of you, bestie." Mateo smiled in approval. "That's right. All for one and one for all?"

"Whatever." A message vibrated on Sid's phone. He rubbed a hand over his face and stared out the window.

Even though they were running for their lives, Alexa couldn't help the warmth spreading through her chest each time she glanced back at Sid. Of all the people in the world to join her on an insane adventure, it had to be him.

Mateo must have noticed her grin. He nudged her knee and gave her a knowing smile, tossing a nod in Sid's direction. Alexa suppressed her smile but let herself enjoy the brief moment of happiness.

Heading south toward Rochester, Alexa was glad for the *Spacehog* song playing over her satellite radio. She let the sailing opening riff swell and break over her body. Everything would be okay.

Yes, everything would be okay.

Chapter Thirteen

AS THEY EMERGED FROM the other side of the Twin Cities, they developed a flimsy cover story. They agreed to provide their parents with only as much information as absolutely necessary. Alexa worried someone might have reported her reckless driving to the local authorities. Hopefully, no one got her license plate number or caught a video on her phone.

Una continued to direct them south toward Mankato, Minnesota, until they joined I-90 in the south end of the state. The urban centers fell away as they entered a world of rolling hills and cornfields.

Once Mateo had cleared what he could with his mother, he texted Alexa's parents on her behalf as they continued along the interstate. In a series of brief messages, he explained that something had come up, a friend needed their help, and Alexa accidentally left her phone behind. Naturally, Cynthia wanted to know whose Subaru sat in their driveway and when they planned to return. Mateo replied, *We'll let you know as soon as we can.*

Alexa's parents didn't care for that response.

Sid maintained a mad text exchange with his parents, his face growing grimmer with each phone vibration. After the hundredth text somewhere outside of New Ulm, he let out a loud, extended groan and muttered something about McDonalds.

At sunset, they stopped at a gas station. Alexa's bladder and aching hands couldn't take it anymore. Everyone but Una had missed dinner, and the gas light blinked as they took the nearest off-ramp. Their only option was an isolated, two-pump station in the middle of nowhere.

The three teenagers hopped out of the Honda in a daze. Sid volunteered to pump the gas, and Mateo offered to pay. Una stretched out beneath the giant blanket in the backseat, horn glinting in the gas station's fluorescent lights.

Alexa rubbed her cold arms and walked up to the wilted gas station. Of course, she had forgotten to grab a jacket before running for her life, along with Sid. Mateo had his oversized hoodie, which was hardly enough for a late fall evening.

The gas station's interior was as miserable as the exterior, reeking of old fry grease and motor oil.

"Excuse me, where's the restroom?" Alexa asked the ancient cashier, who was picking at her nails.

"Back and to the right." The older woman rubbed her watery eyes, her voice thick and husky from decades of smoking. "You got to hold down the handle so the toilet flushes right."

The women's room was as feared—dirty and smelling of urine. Under different circumstances, she would have turned around and walked out of such a disgusting place. The lightbulb over the sink flickered a staccato rhythm. The hand drying device, a long and greasy loop of cotton towel, was piled into a heap on the floor.

Wincing throughout the whole process, Alexa did what she came to do. After emptying her bladder, she assessed her hands. The bandages hung from her fingers in a frayed mess, but at least she wasn't bleeding through them anymore. They needed to be replaced. Alexa doubted she would find what she needed at the gas station.

Cleaning her hands as best she could, Alexa gazed into the smeared mirror. Shadows hung beneath her eyes, and her pale complexion looked more ghost than human.

"We're doing this," Alexa scolded her reflection, clutching and unclutching her damp, tender hands. "We'll go as far as we need to, for Una's sake."

Her reflected face pulled an unconvincing grin, then faded into the truth: a girl scared out of her mind. Her stomach gurgled. She might be terrified, but she needed to eat something.

Alexa left the bathroom and found Mateo with a stack of junk food and drinks at the register. Outside, Sid leaned against her Civic, face turned to the sky and eyes closed. His handsome face relaxed for a moment, and he was at peace. The moment ended when he reached into his back pocket and tugged out his phone. His expression told Alexa all she needed to know.

"You look tired, Lex." Mateo gave Alexa a gentle nudge as he paid for their pile of snacks.

"Gee, thanks." Alexa waved her mess of tattered bandages. "I need to fix this at some point. Don't want to get an infection on top of everything else."

"Do you think you can wait until morning? I'd feel better if we put as much distance between us and that cloud monster beastie."

"Totally agree," Alexa said. "The farther, the better."

Mateo and Alexa piled the bags of chips, packages of snack cakes, and three sensible bottles of water into their arms and headed out. A cold blast of fall greeted her. She swore the temperature had dropped five degrees during their time in the convenience store's humid warmth.

Mateo volunteered to sit next to Una for the next leg of the drive. As Alexa expected, Una squirmed and complained when Mateo carefully pushed Una's legs aside to make room. Mateo took up much less space than Sid, but that didn't stop the unicorn from making a fuss.

The things I do just to stay alive, Una grumbled. *Alexa Baxter, could you please uncover my head? I cannot stand this any longer.*

"Sorry, I know it's cramped back there." Alexa pulled down the blanket to reveal Una's delicate head.

The unicorn raised its head and took a quick assessment of the surroundings. *They would never believe me if I told anyone what Earth was like. I did not realize how long it took to get everywhere.*

"Yeah, everything's a bit spaced out in this part of the country."

I shall fight to maintain patience. Una curled its head over its front legs and let the tip of its horn settle into the back of Alexa's seat. That would leave a mark.

"Ready to do this?" Sid dropped into the driver's seat and adjusted his mirrors for the third time.

Mateo shoved a cloven hoof out of his side. "When you are."

Sid pulled out of the gas station, stomping his foot a little too hard on the gas. He stammered his apologies and turned them back toward the interstate. Alexa handed out drinks and treats to everyone. Mateo's phone vibrated in the center cup holder. Alexa angled her head to read the upside-down text from her mother: *Mateo, please tell Alexa to call me immediately when you get this.*

"Crap looks like it's my turn." Alexa shoved a handful of chips into her mouth.

"You got this." Mateo patted her shoulder and ripped open a bag of Cheetos.

So far Sid and Mateo had run the parental gauntlet with mixed results. Mateo and his mom, Pilar, had an extraordinarily trusting relationship. She asked him to contact her every few hours and let her know if he needed her help.

Sid's parents, however, were the complete opposite. From what Alexa had gathered, they were confused, frustrated, and increasingly furious. Their golden boy, who had never done anything irresponsible before, had left his sister to wait, in tears, for someone to pick her up thirty minutes late from dance class.

"But, I'm an adult," Sid had hissed after shoving his phone aside. "I always do everything they ask, and just this one time—just this once they can't let it go. Mom and Dad are on call, so maybe they'll get too distracted to worry."

Alexa wasn't convinced. From the conflicted expression on Sid's face, neither was he.

Una demanded that they keep their exact whereabouts ambiguous without giving an apparent reason for doing so. *Just do not name our location to anyone. Locations can be traced.*

Alexa held Mateo's phone as if it might bite her. "I'm not sure I can do this."

"Yes, you can," Mateo said through a mouthful of Cheetos. "Stay calm, and carry on, my lady in black."

Alexa's heart thrummed wildly in her chest. She hit the SEND button and held her breath as her mother picked up after the first ring.

"Mateo? This better be Alexa." Her mother's commanding voice filled her ear.

"Yeah, it's me." Alexa squeaked.

"What the hell is going on? First, Mateo texts that you're going out for coffee. Then I see you've left your phone behind. You *never* leave your phone behind. I asked him about the car in front of my house, and it's Sidhit Dayani's? But there's no Sidhit to be found anywhere. What's his car doing here, Alexa?"

"We were doing homework?" Alexa said. The anger in her mother's voice left her breathless.

"Where are you?"

"Uh, a friend of ours is in some ... uh ... trouble, and we need to take them out west."

"Dammit, Alexa. Stop being so cryptic. Where are you?" Alexa's mom shouted so loud everyone in the car could hear her.

You cannot tell her our location, Una repeated for the umpteenth time. Alexa turned toward Una, and the unicorn's penetrating gaze met hers. Una's eyes shimmer like miniature galaxies in the car's dim light.

"I'm okay, I promise," Alexa murmured.

"Deflect and reassure," Mateo whispered. "Deflect and reassure."

"Lex, where are you?" Her mother's voice took on a new tone. Fear tangled into her mother's words.

Tears burned Alexa's eyes, catching her off-guard. "We're heading west. A friend needs a ride. We're the only ones that can help." Alexa's throat tightened.

Cynthia's voice softened. "Promise me, you'll be careful."

"Yes, I promise. I'm sorry. I have to go; I'll talk later." Alexa tried to keep her voice steady, but a tremble shook her words. "I love you."

"I love you too, honey."

Alexa ended the conversation, and a sob escaped. The day's intensity pressed against her skull, growing into a headache. She pulled her legs to her chest, cradled her bag of chips, and shoved down another greasy mouthful.

Una lifted its head and gently nudged Alexa with its horn. *There is a monster after us, Alexa Baxter. And I cannot get away without your help. You are the only one who can save me. Please don't give up on me.*

"Of course, I won't," Alexa said between fistfuls of chips. "Any idea how much farther?"

We must continue for a long time. As long as we keep at this pace, I am not worried.

"Great. Then I'm taking a nap. Wake me up if we have to change directions." Alexa poured the chip crumbs down her throat, hiccupped, and turned toward the door. She shifted around until she found a comfortable position. Sleep crept in and laid heavy against her head as the soft tones of Radiohead droned over the speakers.

Chapter Fourteen

ALEXA MUST BE DREAMING.

She sat in her Civic's passenger seat. The world whipped past, rolling in perfect waves beyond her window. The earth was a quilt of dull, lifeless gray grass, and the sky above hung heavy with thick storm clouds.

Sid drove her car, but he looked all wrong. His figure undulated like the landscape, flattening then billowing out behind the steering wheel. Alexa turned to find Mateo in the same state: expanding, contracting, inflating, and deflating.

And Una, where was Una? The unicorn had condensed into a single orb of light and hugged Mateo's ever-changing form.

A roar gathered from beneath Alexa's feet and shook the world. The landscape cowered from the horrible noise, flattening into an endless, shuddering plain. The sky was unleashed, pouring over everything. Soon, the division between sky and earth was replaced by a torrent of writhing clouds, reaching its long fingers into Alexa's car.

Was it the monster? How did it find them?

Alexa braced herself against the door, covering her head for impact.

YOU SHOULD NOT RUN, the voice boomed, obliterating everything. The voice did not come from outside Alexa but from within.

YOU DO NOT UNDERSTAND. The voice slithered into her brain, winding and curling within the curve of her skull.

"It's a dream, a dream," Alexa gasped, her voice tiny within the surrounding cloud. The blackness in her brain curled down her spine, gripping her ribs.

YOU MUST LISTEN TO US. Black fingers latched around her throat, growing tighter with each breath.

"No, please, stop!" Alexa thrashed in her seat, her hands unable to grip the vines of cloud weaving in and out and around her body.

DO NOT TRUST IT. YOU MUST NOT TRUST IT.

She gasped for air and tried to scream, but the darkness poured down her throat until it oozed from her nose, her ears, and even her eyes. She had to wake up. This couldn't be real. She threw herself against the seat, the window, kicked at the floor, anything to break through the nightmare.

A ray of light broke through.

YOU MUST NOT TRUST IT. Her invader shrunk back, condensing into a tight knot at the front of her skull.

The light cut through the shadows, and Alexa could breathe again. She gasped, gulping pure, unpolluted air, and convulsed awake.

"Alexa?"

Alexa sat up in her seat, rubbing at the crust in her eyes. The world beyond her window was a typical Midwest landscape—an interchanging medley of browns and grays, with the occasional glimmer of yellow or green grass, bowed beneath the blustering wind.

"Alexa, you okay?"

Alexa touched her lips. Rough bandages scraped the tender skin. Where was she? The dream had dissolved, leaving behind a racing pulse and dried tears crusting her cheeks.

"Did you have a nightmare?"

Alexa turned from the window, rearranged her twisted seat belt, and met the tired eyes of the boy she adored. Everything returned in a rush. Una. Mateo. Sid. The monster. They were running for their lives.

"You were kinda jerking all around in your sleep." Sid yawned and blinked away his exhaustion.

"Yeah, it was a crazy dream." Alexa's yawn matched Sid's.

Had he driven all night? Where were they? Alexa scanned the highway billboards for information. The dashboard read seven in the morning. She had slept for almost eight hours. She must have needed to rest more than she realized. Saving a unicorn was exhausting work.

Alexa turned to the back seat and snickered at what she found. At some point, Una had placed its head in Mateo's lap, and a gentle snore rose from its palpating nostrils. The tip of the unicorn's horn was stuck several inches into the back of Alexa's seat. Mateo's head had fallen back, and a thin trickle of drool slid from the corner of his slack mouth.

"Adorable," Alexa giggled. "How are you, Sid? Anything happen while I was out?"

"Not much," Sid shrugged and yawned again. "We pulled over at a rest stop around midnight and let Una stretch its legs. Well, we didn't have much of a choice. Una was being a real brat, so we had to stop. Luckily, it was midnight in the middle of nowhere, and we didn't run into anyone.

"Mateo fell back asleep. I got gas halfway across South Dakota. I napped at three in the morning at a different rest stop. So far, no sign of monsters."

"So, just a normal Monday night, eh?" Alexa laughed.

"Yep, nothing too interesting."

The early morning traffic was sparse on the interstate. No one seemed in a hurry, and was close enough to notice a unicorn passed out in the back.

"We're not too far from Rapid City." Sid jerked his chin to one of the passing billboards. "I thought it might be nice to get a decent breakfast. And you know that truck-stop coffee is strong enough to kill a mule."

"Sounds awesome. I can take the wheel, and you can get more sleep."

"Speaking of driving ..." Sid grinned his sexy crooked grin. "You were pretty impressive back there."

"Oh, you mean when we ran from the monster?" Alexa blushed. "It's not a big deal."

"Uh, it kinda is. Taking the bike path and cutting across a playground? You didn't hesitate, not even once. You're a badass."

"I like driving, I guess." Alexa's cheeks heated further.

"Maybe sometime you'll have to show me how you do it." Sid tossed Alexa another crooked grin.

Warmth spread from her cheeks to her chest, and her ears rang. Give Sid a driving lesson? "Okay, sure. Why not?"

Sid's cell phone started vibrating in the cupholder nearest him. Sid glanced down, gnawed his bottom lip, and rubbed his temple.

"How's the parental situation?" Alexa asked. She never thought she would be grateful to have left her cell phone several states away.

"Mateo's doing fine, but I'm in deep shit." Sid smiled despite the grave expression on his face. "We'll be lucky if they don't set off an Amber Alert."

"Can they do that?" Alexa's eyes widened. She pictured a swarm of police cars, lights blazing, racing across South Dakota to catch up with them. What happened if they stopped for too long? Would the monster catch up with them? What would a bunch of cops do when they laid their eyes on Una?

An odd tingle squirmed beneath Alexa's forehead. She immediately scratched it, thinking she had some stray hairs clinging to her brow. Nope, nothing. The weird sensation disappeared as quickly as it arrived. It must be from all the stress.

"No, I'm just being dramatic." Sid rubbed the back of his neck and stretched his back as best he could while driving. "We're eighteen, right?"

"Mateo's still seventeen, but his mom would never do that. I'm more worried about our parents."

"I bet they're already on a first-name basis," Sid said. "I'm in so much trouble."

"I'm sure I am too." Alexa sighed, recalling the fear in her mother's voice during last night's call. Her stomach rumbled, demanding coffee and food. "Stopping for breakfast sounds nice. Maybe that's just what we need to get through whatever happens today."

"I'll keep a lookout for a truck stop with a cafe." Sid yawned a third time.

Alexa glanced out the rear window and smiled into the cloudless pale blue sky. There were no monsters on their tail as far as she could see. The unicorn twitched in its sleep, and Mateo twitched in response. Alexa wouldn't wake them until necessary.

According to a passing road sign, they were still twenty miles from Rapid City. Alexa had never been on a multi-state road trip before. Her parents preferred flying as much as humanly possible, so Alexa's only experience on the open road was from books and movies. Something about crossing a state she had never crossed made her heart sing with possibility. The rational part reminded her this wasn't some romantic adventure. They were running for their lives.

"I'm so sorry to drag you into this," Alexa said. She would never forget the horrible sounds the cloud monster made.

"Half of me is completely freaked out," Sid said. "Sometimes I feel like I'm losing my mind. I've never felt like that before. Everything in my life has been so ... according to schedule. I follow a fairly routine, and everything works out how I expect. I've never done anything reckless before."

Alexa let out a hollow laugh. "Yeah, me too. I know I'm a bit ... unique, but I'm also the same as you. My life was pretty boring before I met Una."

The last two days were an absolute fever dream. What would that day bring? Hopefully good weather, open roads, and finding Una's "Rift" before the end of the day. The strange itch between her eyes tingled again. She rubbed it away and enjoyed snatching glances at Sid's profile. Another big yawn stretched his face. He needed to get off the road sooner than later.

"The next time you see a sign for a gas station with a travel center, let's get off there," Alexa suggested. "You need to rest."

"I sure do," Sid said through another yawn. "Pancakes sound delicious right now."

The great plains beyond them began to rise and fall as distant low mountains appeared. The wind picked up speed, hurling at her Civic. Alexa would have a long, blustery day of driving ahead of her.

Alexa woke Mateo and Una with a light shake of their feet. Mateo was typically slow to wake. He frowned, stretched, and then immediately fell back asleep. Unlike Mateo, Una woke immediately, clear blue eyes alert and vivid as the morning sky.

I slept longer than I meant to sleep. Where are we, Alexa Baxter?

"A town called Rapid City. And sorry, but I need to cover you up again before you blind someone. We're about to stop to get breakfast, so I'll try to find some more macaroni and cheese for you. I would be surprised if they didn't have something like it at a truck stop."

Do you mean the shell food? Lovely. I would very much appreciate that. The unicorn turned down its mouth as Alexa dumped the blanket back over its luminous body.

But do not stay for long. We still have far to go.

Chapter Fifteen

THEY PULLED OFF AT the next travel center. Bleary-eyed and yawning, Sid parked in the lot outside the diner portion of the truck stop.

Alexa opened her door, underestimating the power of the wind, which nearly ripped her door from her fingers.

"Oh, whoa." Sid snickered as an actual tumbleweed drifted across the parking lot.

"Guess we're not in Kansas anymore, kids." Mateo winked from the backseat and shoved open his door. "I need coffee."

Alexa held open her door and said to Una, "Don't worry. We should be in and out. These places always have speedy service."

Waste no time. I have an odd feeling about this place. Una stretched out across the back seat with a satisfied sigh. *And please remember the shell food.*

"Of course!" Alexa heaved her door closed. Cold and hungry, she stiffened against another wind gust and stumbled toward the restaurant. Sid jumped ahead of them and held open the restaurant doors. Mateo and Alexa hurried through, hand in hand, each making jokes about Dorothy and the Wicked Witch of the West.

The alluring smell of greasy food and cinnamon perfumed the diner's warm air. The truck stop was huge. Alexa peered down a wide hallway to her left, leading to the bathrooms and a giant convenience store. Hopefully, it was big enough to have a decent first aid section so she could replace her bandages and maybe grab a warm sweatshirt.

The diner's decor was country chic—lots of wood paneling and beige-textured walls. Colorful paintings of pastoral scenes hung everywhere. A large glass case at the front counter displayed pies and pastries. A tired waitress, possibly coming off the night shift, leaned against the register as she scanned her phone, ignoring the wind-swept teens.

Alexa couldn't say why, but something about the place unnerved her. The itch beneath her forehead quivered, and her gut warned her to pay attention and be wary.

Sid's face split into a yawn so huge he lost his balance and stumbled into Alexa. Alexa's cheeks flared as she caught him. She had only touched him once before. Her hands ached in both pain and pleasure. Sid sleepily apologized and righted himself. Mateo smirked and shot Alexa a look.

A kind-eyed waitress approached to seat them. She had the agreeable composure and build of a quintessential Midwestern waitress: a little thick in the middle, a cloud of honey-blonde hair, and a sassy twinkle in her eye.

"Oh, my, on the road all night?" The waitress beamed as she scanned the teenagers.

"Yes. Table for three, please," Alexa said as Mateo shrugged in response, and Sid held himself up by leaning against the partition between the front counter and the diner.

The waitress led them into a booth where everyone ordered a round of coffee. Alexa tried to make up for her companion's garbled requests with excessive politeness and a wide smile.

"I'll bring a whole pot." Their waitress, Debbie, winked before disappearing in a puff of floral perfume.

"Do you think Una'll be okay out there?" Alexa twisted in her seat. She should have sat facing the door.

"It's too early in the morning for anyone to notice anything," Mateo grumbled as his phone vibrated. "Oh, hey. I gotta check in with Mom. Can you please order blueberry pancakes for me if the server comes back? Extra syrup?"

"I got you." Alexa scrutinized the menu. She was pleased to see they sold everything on the menu all day. Unfortunately, they didn't have macaroni and cheese. "Do you think fettuccine alfredo is a good substitute for mac and cheese?"

"I'm not a unicorn, so I wouldn't know." Sid snorted, amused by his own joke. "Oh, yeah, they have breakfast sandwiches. And, oooh, omelets..."

"What if it isn't safe for us to stop?" Alexa's voice arched into an ear-piercing screech near the end of the question.

Sid winced and covered his ears. "Wow, you've got a dog whistle on you. It's going to be fine. A proper meal's worth the stop."

"Sorry." Alexa slumped in her seat; cheeks hot. "It happens when I'm nervous."

Sid shook his hair out of his eyes and grinned. "You're nervous a lot."

Alexa pressed her cold hands to her hot face. "Yeah ... can't help it."

"I never get to eat food like this at home. I'm sort of excited." Sid bounced in his seat. "Cheese, bacon, eggs, *and* ham? Mom would never let me order that."

"So, you get boring, healthy food at home like I do?" She had decided to order a classic breakfast platter for the same reason. Cynthia hadn't allowed real bacon in the house for years.

"My sister's nanny usually cooks for us." Sid winced. "Don't judge."

Nannies, personal chefs, and housekeepers were common enough in Riverview. Alexa knew Sid's mom was a nationally renowned cardiothoracic surgeon; his father was another surgeon at a big hospital in the Cities. His family lived in one of the stately mansions dotting the river bluffs overlooking the St. Croix River.

Alexa said, "So, what does she cook?"

"A little bit of everything. Maria is the best. She's been around since I was small, too. Love her. No big surprise, she's been around more than the parental units."

"Oh, sure." Alexa realized she might be lucky to have parents who managed to make time for their children despite their busy schedules.

"Done and done!" Mateo flopped back into the booth beside Alexa. "Of course, Cynthia reached out to my mom and got her a little worked up. But, I've talked her off the cliff." He handed his phone to Alexa. "You need to text your mom so she'll stop blowing up my phone."

"Just tell her I'm fine, don't worry, and I'm sorry." Alexa ought to call her mom, too, but she didn't have the energy for it between worrying about Una and the nagging sensation that something wasn't quite right.

After Debbie left with their orders and a big pot of coffee, the three teenagers lapsed into silence. The coffee was surprisingly good. Alexa and Mateo slurped their drinks while Sid fought to keep his eyes open.

"Oh, and more good news." Mateo waved his phone. "I looked at the Riverview police blotters before I fell asleep last night. Somehow, no one called the cops on us. But also, there were no reports of a lightning-and-thunder monster, which confirms what Una said. We can only see it because it's hunting us."

Alexa shivered and scratched at her forehead. Hopefully, they would never see that awful monster again.

"That's so messed up." Sid sat up and rubbed his red-rimmed eyes. "How is that possible? That thing was so loud and huge. My ears were literally ringing when we first hit the interstate."

"We left reality a few hundred miles ago." Alexa twisted a piece of frayed bandage, exposing healing scratches.

"We sure did." Sid dropped his head back and closed his eyes.

Alexa allowed her gaze to wander in his direction. Would she ever stop feeling a little flutter in her stomach whenever he entered a room? The dark fringe of his eyelashes kissed the top of his cheeks, and a lock of hair fell across his smooth forehead. He didn't even have pimples.

Sid's eyes flashed open as if he could feel her stare. "What?"

"Sorry, I zoned out for a second." Alexa dropped her head and tugged her stocking cap lower on her brow. Mateo kicked her beneath the table, and she caught the edge of his knowing grin.

Sid was about to say something else, but their orders had arrived. They are like men at their last meal—ravenous but occasionally queasy. The warm Styrofoam to-go box of fettuccine alfredo arrived as they devoured their last few bites. Debbie commended their appetites and left the check behind. They paid with Sid's cash and left a good tip.

They headed to the rest stop's convenience store section to grab additional snacks and fresh bandages for Alexa. She found what she needed and ended up near a rack of sweatshirts in the touristy section of the store. An oversized black sweatshirt with a wolf howling at the moon in front of the words: Black Hills National Forest drew her eye. Sid caught her admiring the shirt in the small mirror attached to the rack and offered to purchase it.

Alexa shook her head and was about to hang the sweatshirt back up when Sid snatched it from her hands. "You need it. It's cold outside."

Alexa accepted his gift and gratefully pulled the warm, oversized shirt over her head as she headed to the bathroom to wash her hands and apply fresh bandages. The truck stop's bathroom was a vast improvement from the last place in southern Minnesota. In the mirror, she looked better than the last time she had studied her reflection.

A bit at a time, Alexa removed the dirty, torn bandages. Her fingers looked better than expected—pink and healing. Her palms were a little worse for wear. One particularly angry cut split the center of her left palm.

Hands re-wrapped, stomach full of breakfast, and sporting a cozy sweatshirt, Alexa was ready to take on another difficult day. Sid would get some rest, Mateo would keep them motivated, and she would be the only one to hear Una's string of complaints. Maybe they could do this after all? Maybe they would find the Rift Una was looking for that very day.

Leaving the bathroom, Alexa plowed into the soft cushion that was Debbie. The waitress stood on the other side of the door. Alexa stuttered an apology, but Debbie didn't move out of her path. Debbie's once cheerful eyes had dulled into a thousand-yard state.

"Hey, sorry. Debbie?" Alexa paused, unsure whether to push past the waitress or wait for a response.

Debbie blinked and fixed Alexa with a cold, intense glare.

Alexa flinched away. Somehow, Debbie wasn't Debbie anymore.

Chapter Sixteen

"DEBBIE, ARE YOU—"

Without warning, Debbie lunged and grabbed Alexa's shoulders. A thick grunt escaped her slack lips as she shoved Alexa against the wall. Alexa didn't have time to brace herself, and her head bounced off the hard, textured surface. The decorative chair rail dug into her back, knocking the wind out of her.

"Oh, whoa, stop," Alexa gasped, stunned by the impact. Her vision blurred. The itching in front of her skull returned. The sensation of hundreds of tiny fingers scraped inside her head. The waitress's pupil dilated, expanded, and turned her eyes completely black.

"Jesus, effing Christ." Alexa batted Debbie's arms.

"You must stop." The waitress pressed her round face near Alexa's. Pink lipstick smeared her coffee-stained teeth, and sour breath blew against Alexa's cheek. The black in Debbie's eyes swirled in her sockets.

"Stop? Stop what?"

"*You must stop.*" Debbie's voice was low and expressionless, the pleasant Midwestern twang long gone.

"Get off me!" Alexa squirmed. Her sneakers squeaked against the tile, searching for purchase. Was Debbie holding her above the floor? Where was Mateo? Sid? They must have gone to the car.

"YOU. MUST. STOP." Debbie repeated, knocking Alexa's head against the wall as she uttered each word.

The deep, resonant voice was familiar, like the voice from her nightmare hours before. The sort of voice that seeped into her head grabbed hold and threatened to strangle all sense and reason.

"YOU MUST STOP RUNNING."

"Put me down." Alexa slapped at Debbie's thick arms. They seemed made of stone.

"YOU DO NOT UNDERSTAND. YOU DO NOT KNOW WHAT YOU ARE HELPING. YOU CANNOT TRUST THE BRIGHT ONE."

"Una? What the fuck?" The itching beneath Alexa's forehead expanded. The tiny fingers tapped against the back of her eyes. Needles of pain scraped backward toward her spine.

"LISTEN TO ME." Debbie's jowls jiggled. A flash of electric green threaded across the waitress's black eyes.

"What's going on back here?" An authoritative voice barked from the end of the hallway.

Debbie's hands dropped to her side, releasing Alexa. Her head also dropped, face blank, eyes closed. Alexa clung to the walls as she slid away from the waitress, her sneakers squeaking as she regained her balance.

"Debbie, what the hell has gotten into you?" A bald man clopped down the hall with a button-up shirt and nametag that screamed manager. He turned to Alexa, confused and horrified. "Miss, are you all right? This is—-Debbie must not be in her right mind. Too many doubles, I told her ... Do you ... uh ... want to file a complaint? Or can I give you a refund? Or a gift card?"

Alexa wavered, holding to the wall for dear life. What had just happened? She shook everywhere, little spurts of fear igniting her senses. Everything was too loud, too bright. She wanted to collapse on the floor and curl into a ball until everything disappeared.

"Lex?" Mateo appeared in front of her, face stricken, breathing hard. "We have to get out of here."

"What happened?" Mateo and Alexa asked each other in unison.

"The monster," Mateo replied. "It's here. It's coming."

"Yeah, I think I knew that."

"What?"

Alexa took Mateo by the hand. "Run."

Skidding on fleshly mopped floors, Mateo and Alexa hop-skipped out of the diner. The moment they burst out of the building, a gale of wind knocked them sideways.

They found Sid staring at the sky, half in and half out of the car, eyes wide with horror. Una had tossed aside its blanket and was also staring at the sky with wide eyes. There was no time to tell the unicorn to get back under cover. Nor time to reflect on Debbie's violent behavior.

"Go, go, go," Alexa shouted as she raced with Mateo to her Civic.

Mateo tossed her the car keys. Alexa dumped herself into the driver's seat, and her companions piled in. In a panic, Una jammed its horn into the ceiling as Sid made himself room in the backseat. The unicorn shrieked, and Sid reached towards Una's horn.

"Don't touch Una's horn. That's how I got these!" Alexa waved a bandaged hand, secured her seatbelt, and threw the car into reverse. "Hang on, everyone."

Alexa didn't need to look into the sky to know the monster was on their heels. She raced the Honda across the truck stop parking lot, avoiding cars and people while blowing her horn. Her rearview mirror was once again filled with mounting piles of black clouds. Green lightning veined the roiling mass. Massive tendrils whirled in their direction as if trying to pluck them from the road.

A too-familiar roar rattled the car. Alexa dodged an incoming semi-truck and a couple of guys about to cross into their path. The young men threw Alexa several vulgar gestures as she skipped a stop sign and turned onto the road leading them back to the interstate.

"Where are we going, Una?" Alexa barked. She paused at a red light and jammed the gas when no one came in the other direction.

South! We must go south.

"Got it." Alexa merged onto the interstate. In her mirror, the monster was already growing smaller.

With a bang and a squeal, Una freed itself from the roof and fell into Sid's lap. The boy and the unicorn wrestled to find space to fit both their bodies.

"Well, at least it's a small hole." Mateo peered into the roof's whistling puncture wound.

Alexa ignored the damage to her car and took the bypass, heading south off the interstate. The speed limit was too slow for her taste, and traffic had thickened since they had last cruised the interstate. Ordinary people went about their ordinary day while the cloud monster continued to fade into the background.

"I knew something was off." Alexa rubbed her forehead. The itching had subdued the moment Debbie's eyes turned black. What was causing the strange sensation, and did it have something to do with the monster?

Mateo sagged in the passenger seat and blew a long, low whistle. Sid adjusted Una's forelegs so they draped over his lap. Una turned back its ears and snapped its teeth at Sid's hands.

Sid drew back. "You know I'm just trying to help? Right? Stop being such a princess."

All this Earth slang and jargon. I detest it.

"That was super close." Mateo pressed a hand to his flushed face. "Let's not do that again, okay?"

Every time Alexa glanced into her rearview mirror, the monster continued to recede. "Damn right. Woof. Fast food only from now on."

They flew past clustering suburbia and a warehouse district as the flowing prairie became cluttered by trees and distant mountains. The monster's reappearance, however brief, had left everyone shell-shocked. The two boys stared out the back window as the monster faded from view. Una rested its head between the two seats, breathing in quick, sharp bursts.

The itching beneath her forehead returned once the monster disappeared behind the horizon. The back of her head throbbed from Debbie bouncing her head off the wall. She touched the two tender points of discomfort and shivered. She opened her mouth to tell everyone her personal nightmare, but nothing came out. How could she put Debbie's attack and the weird feelings under her skin into words?

Keep heading south, Alexa Baxter. Una's directions led them down and around the center of Rapid City. The Black Hills beckoned to the west. The swelling plains returned along with the persistent wind. And the monster had disappeared from sight.

"I think we're in the clear," Alexa said, allowing herself to appreciate the lovely mountain view. As her heartbeat returned to a regular rhythm, she took note of each of her injuries. Her hands weren't as bad as yesterday but now she had a persistent headache. She should have grabbed some aspirin with her bandages.

"Everyone okay?" Mateo surveyed the car.

"Yeah, I guess." Sid rested his head against the backseat and yawned.

Una switched its tail but said nothing.

Mateo pouted. "I guess no more breakfasts."

"Yeah, only quick stops when we need them," Alexa agreed. "And we can't stop for a nap. We'll have to rotate drivers every time we fill up with gas. You know what that means, Mateo?"

"Ugh, yeah." Mateo flopped in his seat. "I'll do my best. But you know how I hate driving on the interstate."

Alexa gave him a playful punch in the shoulder. "I believe in you."

As they drove further, Alexa couldn't stop thinking about Debbie's black eyes or the nightmare from earlier. That voice, both the one in her dream and the one coming out of possessed Debbie, seemed to be the same. What did that mean? This monster was more complicated than Una had let on.

"Okay, something wild happened to me at the truck stop." Alexa glanced at Una, who had settled its head between the front seats.

"What? When?" Mateo said.

"After I went to the bathroom, our waitress, Debbie, attacked me."

Sid shook awake. "Wait, what?"

"Super nice waitress Debbie?" Mateo said.

"Yep." Alexa cleared her throat. She couldn't let her emotions overtake her. She needed to sound as reasonable as possible so they would believe her. "Debbie came up and shoved me against the wall. She wasn't acting normal. Her eyes were all screwed up, and her voice was super strange."

Una said nothing, but its ears were pricked forward.

"She did what?" Mateo's eyes widened with a new sort of alarm.

"This is going to sound wild, but I think the monster possessed Debbie somehow." Alexa watched and waited for Una to respond.

"Is that even possible?" Sid turned his tired eyes to Una.

Una didn't respond.

"Okay, just—let me get this clear." Mateo splayed his hands above his head. "Our very nice waitress Debbie attacked you because she was possessed by the cloud monster? Holy shit. Did she, like, say anything?"

Alexa hesitated. "Not really." If Una kept vital information from them, she would return the favor. "She told me we needed to stop running, which makes sense if the monster possessed her. Is that possible, Una? Why didn't you mention this before?"

I am sorry, Alexa Baxter, but there are things I am not allowed to tell you. There are specific mandates between Earth and the multiverse. You should not know I even exist.

"You're not answering my question, Una." Alexa's shoulder slumped.

I also did not know many things about the monster. I knew they were brutal and efficient, but I did not realize they could divide themselves. This also troubles me.

"You must know more than that? Please, anything else?" Alexa begged.

I am sorry, Alexa. All I know is that I underestimated the monster. We must be more cautious of strangers. And we must go faster. Stop as little as possible.

Alexa swallowed her frustration and clutched the steering wheel. Something about Una's calm, steady reply belied the spark of fear in the unicorn's eyes. What was the Bright One keeping from them?

"Lex, what did Una say?" Mateo said.

Alexa chewed her inner cheek. "Una doesn't know what's going on either. And we need to keep going."

"Seriously?"

"That's what the unicorn said." Alexa shrugged, pressing her lips tight to keep from letting out her frustrations.

The Bright One. Una's nostrils flared.

"Sorry, that's what *the Bright One* said."

"Are you keeping something from us?" Mateo snapped and clapped his hands near Una's head. "Are you even paying attention?"

Una raised its head and laid back its ears. *Alexa Baxter, please tell Mateo not to ever do that again.*

"Una, we're all frustrated." Alexa's hands gripped the steering wheel so hard that the pain in her palms flared. "And we're risking our lives for you. Are you sure there's nothing else you can tell us?"

The chain of correspondence annoyed Alexa, and yet she was glad. If the other two knew all of Una's responses, Mateo would read the unicorn the riot act, and who knew what Sid might do? Keeping everyone alive and safe had to be Alexa's top priority.

Una looked Alexa in the eye, blue eyes shining. *Please try to trust me. I know you are all overwhelmed. There is only so much I can explain. The multiverse beyond this place is very complicated.*

Alexa sighed and rolled her shoulders. "Fine, whatever. Una asks us to trust it, and I guess that's all we can do right now."

Mateo folded his arms over his chest. "That's not acceptable."

Una bared its teeth. *You must accept it.*

"Whatever, everybody. I just want to get some sleep." Sid raised the to-go container from the diner and waved it toward the unicorn. "You want some breakfast?"

Una immediately perked up, tail swishing beneath the blanket.

"That must be a yes." Sid opened the container, and Una immediately shoved its muzzle into the saucy noodles.

"This is too much." Mateo banged his head against his headrest. "I just say we do what we gotta do. Get Una to wherever it needs to go and go home. The monster will stop chasing us when you're gone, right?"

Una paused between mouthfuls of fettuccine. *Yes, of course. You will mean nothing to the monster once I am gone.*

Alexa frowned at the unicorn. "Promise?"

Yes. I promise.

Chapter Seventeen

THE WORLD FLATTENED again and revealed a cloudless sky. The change in landscape made Alexa ache for her sketchbook and pencils. She would have placed the tip of her pencil on the side of the sketchbook, keeping a light hand to indicate the delicate line between land and sky. Once the horizon was in place, a sharp, soft-leaded pencil would help her accentuate the contrast between the prairie grass and the unblemished heavens.

Alexa didn't mind driving while everyone else in the car dozed. However, a knot of pain had gathered between her shoulders, and her hands started itching again. She took turns rubbing each palm against the steering wheel. Her eyes ached from staring into the bright sky—the things she would do for some cortisone cream and a cheap pair of sunglasses.

Beside her, Mateo twitched and mumbled in his sleep. Sid had succumbed to exhaustion once they crossed into Wyoming, and not even a restless unicorn disturbed his slumber. Una also slipped in and out of sleep, waking to give Alexa adjustments to their travel path every hour or so.

Between her back and her hands, she didn't notice the twinge growing beneath her forehead until the pain grew more pronounced. Without knowing why, she understood the sensation's origin. After driving a couple hundred miles, her favorite playlist grooving softly in the background, she grew to accept that the monster had something to do with her discomfort. A growing fear tingled up and down her arms. Instead of crying, she gnawed on her lips, praying as each mile passed that the sensation might disappear.

Alexa attempted to distract herself by paging through several of Mateo's playlists. Even though they had wildly different musical tastes, they shared all their playlists with each other. She stuck with her favorite 90's grunge hits. First, the Cranberries, then cleansed the palette with an Alice in Chains dirge but often circled back to her favorites: Nirvana and the Smashing Pumpkins. She lost herself for a brief moment in a Spacehog song until Una's horn glinted from the backseat and returned to her impossible reality.

"You know, I barely know anything about you." Alexa's eyes connected with the dozing unicorn. "Tell me something, anything about Bright Ones. Where are you from? How long have you been running? Anything?"

Very well. Una shook aside the blanket draped over its head. *My people have been nomads for as long as we can remember. We lost our home long ago and have yet to find its replacement. Unfortunately, we are vastly different from the rest of the multiverse. No one will accept us.*

"And the monster. What is that all about?"

Because we are unacceptable, certain entities seek to have us destroyed. The multiverse does not like our power or our society. We refuse to follow their rules, so they have decreed that each and every one of us must be eliminated. So, we run, hoping someone will accept us as we are and give us shelter—a home.

Alexa shook her head and muttered. "If I hadn't seen you and the monster ... I mean, a multiverse? Just crazy."

Perhaps crazy to a simple, isolated Earth creature. There is a reason you do not know what lies beyond. Your people are much too primitive.

Alexa laughed. "Need I remind you that this 'primitive' is trying to save your life?"

Yes, you are right. Una bowed its head. *I must apologize. I do not mean to be rude. Fear has made me coarse.*

"I forgive you. So, can you describe this, uh, pull you feel from the Rift? What does that feel like? How do you know which direction to go?"

Another reason we are mistrusted is that, as the Bright Ones, we are attuned to the energy of the multiverse no matter where we go. This is how I have eluded the monsters. I feel the pull no matter where I go. That is how I found the door to this world.

"Do you know where the next Rift might take you?"

I do not know. Hopefully, this time, I will find a world where I can stay—a world where the monster cannot find me. I thought all the doors to this class of planet were cut off long ago. Of all the thousands of places I could end up ... the multiverse works in mysterious ways.

Alexa rubbed the faint tingle beneath her skull. "How can you communicate with me and no one else?"

For some reason, your brain is amenable to this form of communication. And, because we speak from mind to mind, there is a natural translation between us. There may be others on this planet who are also amenable. However, doing so would waste too much time and effort. Getting off this world is my top priority.

"And, the other Bright Ones? Is this how you communicate, too? Mind to mind?"

That is enough for now, Alexa Baxter. Una let out a long, deep sigh. *I have already told you too much. While I do not agree with most of the universal multiverse policies, I agree that Earth should know little of what exists beyond.*

"Yeah, sure, whatever," Alexa grumbled. She had so many more questions, but agitating Una would wake Sid, and he needed to get his rest.

More miles sped by. The wind had picked up again the further they drove into Wyoming. Air whistled at various pitches through the hole in her Civic's ceiling. How was she ever going to explain that to her parents? Or the half-dozen holes punctured into the back of her seats? She would worry about that once Una found its door and the monster was gone.

Una directed them off the highway and toward another interstate. They needed gas, and a giant travel center sat beside their onramp. Alexa pulled to the nearest gas pump and tossed the blanket back over Una's head.

"I got to pee," Alexa said to Una. "And stretch my legs. We'll only stay for a minute."

Very well, do not stay long.

"What about you? Do you need to use the—uh—facilities?"

I do not defecate the way you do. My body is constructed in a very efficient manner.

"Well, good for you." Alexa nudged Mateo's knee. "I must pee. Can you get us some gas?"

Mateo nodded and yawned in reply. Sid stirred in the back seat, blinking into the afternoon sunlight.

Alexa didn't wait for the boys. Her bladder screamed for relief. They entered when she was already finished, still rubbing the sleep from their eyes. The cool temperature goose-pimpled her skin. She turned her face toward the wind and took a few big breaths while stretching her arms and back.

Although the monster wasn't anywhere in sight, the itching in her brain returned with a vengeance. An ice-cold talon was carved into the front of her brain, pricked across the top of her head, and sent an unpleasant quiver down her spine.

That was new.

Alexa pulled off her stocking cap and ran her bandaged hands across her head. Her heart thudded wildly in her chest as she scanned the horizon again. No monster was in sight, but one clawed through her brain instead.

"You okay?" Sid loped back to the Civic. His casual grace mesmerized Alexa. The wind whipped his thick black hair. How she would love to run her fingers through it.

"I'm fine," Alexa lied and forced a small smile.

"I don't think I've seen you without a hat on," Sid said, flashing his trademark crooked grin.

She blushed and knotted her hat between her fingers. "Yeah, it's sort of an affectation, I admit."

"You have hair," Sid said. He touched a lock of hair curling around her ear for a heart-stopping moment. "Brown. Who would have guessed?"

Alexa hardly breathed as he withdrew his hand. Her cheeks burned, and incredible sensations quivered through her body. She ducked her head, worried he might see how much he affected her. A curious expression crossed Sid's face. She expected him to draw back when he saw her blush. Instead, he leaned back against the Honda and stood beside her, waiting for Mateo to return.

Sid said, "If you had told me on Monday morning I would be in the middle of Wyoming by Wednesday, I would have called you a liar."

Alexa laughed and tugged her knit cap over her head. "If you told me Monday morning I would find a unicorn in the women's bathroom later that day, I would have had you committed."

In response, the icy claws knifed her brain. The weight of her situation immediately swept away any bashful feelings. She balled her hands as Mateo returned.

"You wanna take a round?" Alexa clinked her keys in Mateo's direction.

Mateo blanched. "Ugh ... I'm not ... I guess I could ..."

"I could drive again?" Sid offered.

"Nah, I have at least a few more hours left in me," Alexa said.

"Sid can have shotgun instead?" Mateo waved to the passenger seat.

"Works for me," Alexa said. The distraction of Sid sitting beside her might help her ignore the unwanted sensations tickling her skull. How long could she hide her frightening pokes and itches, and why did it feel necessary to do so?

Alexa hopped into the driver's seat and picked another banger from her grunge mix.

Mateo let out a long, low groan. "When this is over, you're not playing another STP song for the next six months. Got it?"

"You got it." Alexa pulled away from the gas pump and turned them toward the interstate. "Beyonce all day, every day. I promise."

"That's right, you will," Mateo hollered. "And you're coming with me to her next show."

Una let out a long groan. *The noise inside this metal can you call a vehicle is absolutely intolerable. Gods, I hope we find the Rift soon.*

Chapter Eighteen

THEY PLOWED THROUGH the flowing expanse of Wyoming, making good time with Alexa at the helm. Nature called for Sid as they approached a town called Rawlins—a town that reminded Alexa of a home where buffalo roam. They were about to merge back onto the interstate when Una decided it couldn't stand to be stuck in the car one more minute. More than twelve hours had passed since the unicorn last ventured out of the back seat.

Despite being an "advanced being," Una needed to stretch its legs.

They drove through a friendly-looking downtown and cozy neighborhoods. The few people they passed ambled down the sidewalks unhurried, a nice contrast to the intense power walks of Alexa's Riverview neighbors. They rolled around the edge of town, searching for something a little out of the way, with lots of trees and bushes to block Una from view.

Their best bet was a cemetery surrounded by a dense line of trees. A sparse collection of houses lay at a distance to the north and west of the cemetery. No one was parked in the small parking lot, so they found a particularly thick row of hedges and stopped.

Una burst from the car the moment Mateo opened the door. The unicorn kicked its heels, tossed its head, and cantered across the grass. The unicorn dazzled in the afternoon sun on what felt like the world's edge. Watching Una enjoy its momentary freedom reminded Alexa why they ran for their lives.

Their cell phones burst to life when Sid and Mateo hopped out of the car. A duet of groans told Alexa the parents were again making their calls. It was easy to forget reality when so many extraordinary things had happened. Alexa volunteered to watch Una and hurried away in case her mother was on the other side of one of those phones.

From the sound of Sid's voice rising across the grassy knoll, his parents had once again lost their patience. He engaged in an intense conversation, kicking up dried clumps of leaves as he walked rows of headstones. Mateo had positioned himself near the cemetery entrance, watching for traffic or unwanted visitors. From his expression, Mateo's conversation was going better than Sid's. He even cracked a smile once.

Alexa followed in Una's wake. The unicorn's dazzling coat flashed in the afternoon sun's dappled light. The deer-sized creature inspected the grave markers, sneezing at a bouquet of half-dead flowers, and bolted away from a random plastic bag tumbling through the cemetery.

"I know!" Sid shouted from beside a huge marble cross. "Yes? Yes. But I need you to—I can see how you feel that way." He pulled the phone from his ear and performed a series of annoyed gestures before plopping next to a stone angel. "I know ... I know ..."

Is this how you keep your dead? Una appeared beside Alexa and tapped a hoof against a massive granite slab with ADAMS carved across it. This seemed to be a family plot.

"Yeah, one of the ways. But not everyone wants to be buried." Alexa scanned the names nearest to them, most from the previous century.

They are lucky to have a permanent place to rest their bones. Una continued down the line.

"Sure, if you like the idea of six feet of dirt on top of you," Alexa said. "What do Bright Ones do?"

The ceremony is sacred and cannot be shared with anyone who is not a Bright One.

"Right," Alexa grumbled as she passed a cluster of headstones with the last name Turner. Debbie's voice echoed: "You cannot trust it."

Alexa still knew next to nothing about Una. Why did the monster hunt such a small, delicate beast? Sure, the unicorn's horn was as sharp as its tongue. That hardly merited the destruction of a whole species. She rubbed at her forehead. Her skin had grown irritated from all the picking and rubbing. Should she tell Una what was happening to her? Demand and explanation?

Several markers ahead of her, Una paused beside a plot with a large terracotta pot of pink-and-purple pansies. The unicorn gave the flowers a lingering sniff and continued further down the row.

Alexa also paused to read the family names and dates. As she read, the pansies wilted at an unnatural speed. The blooms' color faded, the leaves curled in, and within moments, the flowers were dried-out husks. The faint smell of rot wafted from their withered shapes.

"What the—" Alexa turned toward several other pots of flowers Una had passed and found each one much more dead than when they first arrived. The once-green grass the Bright One had walked upon was covered in blackened hoof prints. The rising scent of decay was oddly familiar.

Cold talons poked deeper than they had before. Alexa cried out, unable to mask her pain any longer. The pain was a burning rod behind her eyes. Pinpricks of light spotted her vision.

Alexa Baxter, are you unwell? Una returned from the nearest mausoleum, dying grass withering behind it.

"No, I'm fine." Alexa gritted her teeth as the pain started to recede.

You look unwell. The unicorn stopped before her, sniffing at her feet.

"Hey, Lex, my mom and your mom both say hi," Mateo yelled from the cemetery entrance. "You should call your mom." He placed his phone to his ear. "See, I told her."

How could she talk to her mom when one monster poked at her brain while another sidled up beside her? Everything was such a mess. She should give up and confess the thing she feared most. Maybe she was wrong. Maybe Una would help her? The unicorn's penetrating gaze caused her to hesitate yet again.

Sid shoved his phone into his pocket. "Yeah, your mom is something else. Everyone is freaking out now. It's only a matter of time before they come after us."

Una stepped in Alexa's path, tail swishing. *We cannot stop. We must keep going.*

"I can't talk to Mom." Alexa pulled her stocking cap further over her brows. At least the pain had receded into her forehead, and the world had stopped blinking in and out. "Let's just keep going. The sooner we get Una on its way, the better. It's too late to stop now."

Yes. You are correct. We draw closer every hour. We will arrive soon.

Mateo said, "Maybe if you talked to her—"

"No, no more talking." Alexa made a bee-line for her car. "Let's keep going. Una thinks we'll arrive soon. We can worry about everything else later."

"Hey, Lex, are you all right?" Mateo reached for her as she buzzed past him.

Alexa dodged his grasp. "Totally. I'm fucking awesome." She glared at Una over the car when she reached the driver's side. "You ready, Bright One?"

Una cocked its head and narrowed its eyes. For a strained moment, the girl and the unicorn stared at each other, neither giving an inch.

Yes, Alexa Baxter. Let us get this over with.

Chapter Nineteen

BEFORE THEY TOSSED the blanket back over Una, Alexa noticed how the unicorn shone brighter than before, as if the Bright One had stuck its tail into an electric socket and recharged. The unicorn practically glowed.

Alexa had solved the mystery of the rotting grass surrounding her parent's shed. Yet another one of the unicorn's many secrets. What else was Una hiding? Luckily, the unicorn couldn't read her mind; she only exchanged wanted communications. And Una wasn't responsible for the prickly presence colonizing the front of her brain.

As the sun lowered in the western sky, its hot globe burned against Alexa's tired eyes. She dreaded the moment she couldn't drive anymore. What would the presence in her mind do once her brain grew idle? The unending road and the ever-shifting landscape gave her something to fixate upon.

Mateo and Sid had begun to notice the change in her behavior. She could feel their eyes upon her as she sang along to her favorite songs. The way they glanced at each other in a silent exchange: a head nod here, a shrug there, told her all she needed to know. They were worried.

Alexa looked in the rearview mirror to see what they saw: red-rimmed eyes, bruise-like shadows hanging beneath them, the way she couldn't stop poking at her forehead. Fear had settled in her gut as the creeping in her brain grew inch by inch. Sheer determination and sing-speaking along to Alice in Chains weren't enough. She wasn't strong enough to hide much longer.

Mateo caught her eyes in the rearview mirror and mouthed for the third time, "What's wrong?"

Alexa shook her head. So many things were wrong; where should she start?

A grim line of determination settled in Mateo's jaw. Alexa knew that look. He wouldn't back down until he got the truth out of Alexa. In the back seat, Sid had grown more and more agitated. He jiggled his knees and chewed his thumbnail. Una raised its head and grumbled silently.

"Hey, Sid," Alexa said. "You're kinda bothering Una."

"Yeah, so what?" Sid glared in the unicorn's direction. "It's bizarre that only you can hear the unicorn. I bet it could talk to us too if it wanted."

Alexa fixed her eyes on the road. "Una said it was too much effort to talk to all of us."

"What is this thing keeping from us?" Sid said. "And what is the unicorn saying you don't want us to know?"

"Nothing. It's nothing. I swear." Alexa wiped a bead of sweat slinking down her brow.

"Lex, I know you're lying." Mateo pursed his lips. "How long have I known you? Please, just tell us."

Should she? What would Una do? "I'm fine. I swear, I'm fine."

"Sure, you are." Sid jostled the unicorn one more time.

I do not like how he is looking at me. Una raised its head and pressed its ears against its skull.

"Hey, let's all just sit back and appreciate nature's beauty, huh?" Alexa gestured to the windows filled with the rising, rocky hills around them. The sky had faded to a lovely pink twilight. Blue mountains rose in the west.

Everyone in the car took a moment to appreciate the landscape.

"It is pretty." Mateo shrugged, glanced at his phone, then looked back to Sid and made a face.

Yep, they were holding a whole other conversation between them. Alexa had suspected as much, but she could hear each phone vibration as the two boys sent text after text to each other.

"So, what kind of story will we give our parents?" Sid pressed his nose to the window. The glass pane fogged beneath his nostrils.

The wind shrieked through the hole in the ceiling. Mateo stuck his pinky into the gap and said, "They'll never believe the truth."

"I hardly believe it, and I'm right here." Sid sat up straighter, once more disturbing Una.

He is doing this on purpose, Una grumbled.

"Oh, stop whining, we're all uncomfortable." Sid's eyes flared, colored by a glint of something wild. "Our parents are all brilliant people and see right through our half-assed bullshit. I don't know how we recover from all this."

Alexa nodded but said nothing. She was sure her parents would be furious once they got home, and this idea worried her almost as much as the monster in her brain.

"Honestly, I don't know if I can deal with this anymore," Sid admitted, unable to look at anyone as he spoke.

"I don't like this either, but it's what we've decided to do," Alexa said.

Stop moving around, you wretched, imbecilic Earth primitive. Una's eyes shone, and its nostrils flared.

Alexa ignored Una. She didn't want to fight, but this argument was a long time coming.

"Who decided?" Sid shoved the unicorn's knees off his lap. "I didn't decide anything. I ran for my life because what the hell else was I going to do? We didn't have a choice."

Mateo frowned. "So, what? You want us to drop you off somewhere?"

Sid shook his head. "No ... I don't know. I'm just in so much shit already. I've never skipped school before."

Mateo said, "Neither have I, but do you see the unicorn sitting next to you?"

"I've tried to be cool until now," Sid said. "Do you know how this could affect my future? I've applied to Harvard and Yale. What if they found out about this? This could ruin my life."

"Ruin your life?" Alexa perked up. "Doesn't that seem a little dramatic?"

Mateo turned in his seat toward Sid. "You know I'm worried too. I'm worried about getting suspended or whatever else might happen. But the monster—"

"What if I get kicked off the soccer team?" Sid said. "I'm going to be grounded until I leave for college. And I'm this close to being valedictorian."

Mateo rolled his eyes. "You mean you might have to go to, what, Northwestern instead of fucking Harvard? Oh, poor you. Your life is so hard."

Una flung the blanket off its head. *What is wrong with these two? Why is everyone so upset?*

"My life has been planned out from birth." Sid pounded a finger into the air. "You don't know my parents. Hell, you don't even know *me*. You're not my friends. What am I doing here?"

Sid's last statement slammed into Alexa's chest. Not even friends? After the previous day and a half?

"Our lives matter too." Mateo's eyes blazed. "Just because I'm the weird queer art kid doesn't mean I don't matter. I'm terrified, too, Sid. I mean, just look at Alexa. My best friend won't tell me what's really going on."

"That's not what I'm saying." Sid shook his hair out of his eyes. "I'm saying it's different. We're different. The pressure I'm under is different. I don't have room to be a screw-up. I never have. I have to be perfect all the damn time."

Mateo shrilled, "You're saying I'm a screw-up?"

Alexa winced in the corner of the car as she fought to concentrate on the road. "Guys, enough. Come on."

Tell them to stop, Alexa Baxter. They are so loud. Why is your Sid so angry?

Alexa laughed. "My Sid ..."

"You don't know me." Sid leaned forward, his face inches from Mateo's. "You don't know how hard I've worked to get where I am."

"You over-privileged king of high school," Sid spat. "You think you work harder than us? Do you even have a job? Do you have a college savings account because you're single-mother can't afford to help you?"

Sid balked. "Well, I—"

"Living in Riverview is the worst when you're poor," Mateo said. "I watch all of you awful rich kids driving your nice cars, wearing your nice clothes, having your picture-perfect future all laid out before you. I work almost twenty hours a week and barely have time to keep up with school and my best friend."

"Guys. Stop." Alexa grew tired of their "who has more to lose" game when they could lose everything. She picked at the sore skin hidden beneath her stocking cap. Yes, they could love absolutely everything, including their lives.

"I don't want this." Sid slumped back into his seat.

"Fine, then we'll dump you at the next gas station," Mateo hissed.

Tell them they better not abandon me. Una slashed its horn through the limited space in the car. *The monster will come for them too. Use them to get to me.*

"Enough!" Alexa shouted, pounding a fist against the steering wheel. "You want to go, Sid? Then go. But I'm all in until this is over. All in. I don't have a choice."

Everyone fell silent. The fight ended for the time being. Alexa's stomach gurgled with hunger, her eyes teared with exhaustion, and the persistent ache between her shoulders was intolerable.

A truck stop came into view.

"I need food and a break," Alexa said.

"Whatever you need, Alexa," Mateo said softly, gently touching her arm.

"Yeah. Sorry. I just—-needed to let that out," Sid said, folding his arms over his chest.

In the east, the sky grew dark. Another long night lay ahead.

Chapter Twenty

THEY HAD FALLEN INTO a routine by the time they reached their next stop. Whoever sat next to the unicorn adjusted Una's blanket if necessary. The driver parked at the pump farthest away from everyone else. Each passenger declared their needs, and those with phones set a ten-minute timer. Then, whoever pumped the gas emptied the leftover garbage from their previous stop.

The moment she parked, Alexa once again raced off to the restroom. Sid stayed to pump the gas and keep an eye on Una. Mateo volunteered to buy dinner from the sandwich shop attached to the gas station. He was also asked to keep an eye out for noodles that might appeal to Una, though Alexa doubted the unicorn needed anything after its lunch of cemetery floral arrangements.

Under the fluorescent glare of the well-lit convenience store, the monster in Alexa's head stuck its sharp claws deep into the front of her skull as she rounded a row of potato chips. She nearly plowed into a woman. The woman, puffy and road-weary, shook her head and muttered something about drug addicts under her breath.

The flashback to the truck stop incident with Debbie caused Alexa to brace herself, fearing another assault. The woman studied Alexa for a heartbeat, seemed to discover something in Alexa's face she found troubling, and walked away, clicking her tongue.

Face aflame, Alexa plunged into the bathroom. She yanked off her hat and attempted to wash her bandaged hands. Icy tines perforated the space just beneath the skull above her eyebrows. A whisper drifted through the empty bathroom.

The monster.

"What are you doing to me?" Alexa whimpered, pressing her fingers around her scratched brow. She wished she would drive her nails into her skull and split it open to remove whatever writhed beneath the surface.

YOU CANNOT STOP US.

Staring into the water swirling down the drain, she couldn't raise her eyes to study her reflection. How did the monster get in her head in the first place? Was it when Debbie attacked her?

"Get out," she murmured, glaring into the faux-granite sink.

TELL US WHERE YOU ARE.

Alexa gripped the edge of the sink. "I won't."

YOU DO NOT KNOW THE PASSENGER YOU CARRY.

Alexa raised her head, taking in a face that had grown ten years older overnight. Her hair stuck up in various directions, and her forehead looked worse than she realized. If she wasn't careful, she might start to draw blood.

The air around her shifted, growing hazy. Swirling tendrils of smoke undulated above her. Another stab right through the center of her frontal lobe caused her to cry out. Her ears rang. She wasn't alone.

"Get out. Please!"

TELL US WHERE YOU ARE.

"You'll kill us if you catch up with us, right?" Alexa gasped. She pressed her palms against her head to stop from rending fingernails against her scalp.

The air thickened, and dark coagulations of mist gathered in the corners of the bathroom. When Alexa looked behind her, away from the mirror, the bathroom appeared normal. The smoke was all in her head.

Another stab lanced her skull. TELL US WHERE YOU ARE.

Alexa sagged against the sink. "No, no, no."

She had to get out of there.

The vague shapes of people moved around her as she exited the bathroom and scrambled for the convenience store's exit. The lights were all too bright. Someone called her name. She didn't stop. Once outside, the evening breeze soothed her hot face, and she whimpered at the slight relief. Brushing away tears and hiccupping sobs, she searched for her car.

The monster's claws loosened. The itching settled as the cool wind lapped her skin. She found her car right where they left it—the pump farthest from all the others. Una would be somewhere in the tangle of blanket in the back seat.

Alexa clenched her hands into aching fists. She wanted to rip open the backdoor and shake answers out of it. But would Una be honest? From the moment she met the Bright One in the bathroom, Una had fed her half-truths.

"Lex?" Sid appeared beside her. He rested a tentative hand on her shoulder. "Something's wrong that you're not telling us."

"I don't know." Alexa whimpered. She couldn't fight the fear of spilling the truth. The truth would change the dynamics of their journey. The goal was simple: get Una to the Rift, outrun the monster while doing it, and deal with their parents once that was over. What would Sid and Mateo do when they discovered the monster not only chased them but also infiltrated Alexa?

"Why won't you tell us?" Sid juggled an armful of caffeine and water for the long night ahead. "What is Una doing to you?"

"It's not Una," Alexa admitted. Voicing the truth would give the monster power.

"What do you mean, Lex?"

"I have this horrible feeling." Alexa walked past her vehicle, simultaneously repelled and drawn to her car and the unicorn in the back seat.

Night had settled into the eastern sky. Alexa couldn't tell if a monster loomed on the horizon. Perhaps it didn't matter now. The monster knew better than to let itself be seen. Her forehead spasmed, and the unseen fingers dug into her gray matter.

"Stop it, go away." Alexa banged at her head with the back of her hand.

"Lex, where are you going?" Mateo called.

Alexa had wandered past the parking lot into the dried grass and dormant shrubbery. She stood on the edge of the frontage road, only two steps from diving into traffic.

"Alexa Baxter!" Mateo screamed.

She shivered and jerked away from the road. Mateo jogged to her side while Sid stood beside her car, lips parted in a silent question.

"Lex, enough of this," Mateo said, grabbing her hand. "Tell me. Please."

"I can't, not yet." Alexa brushed away her tears and fixed a smile on her face. "I just need to rest. That's all."

"That's not all." Mateo's grip tightened. "I know you."

"Please. Let me take a nap. Everything'll be better after I get some sleep."

"Fine." Mateo let her go. "But this isn't over."

Alexa nodded and sniffled. "I know."

Without another word, Alexa headed to the Civic and flopped into the back seat. Una had curled up tight as its body allowed and started to unfurl its legs once Alexa settled. Like an enormous spider unraveling, the unicorn crept toward her. Alexa suppressed a shudder and shoved her fist against her mouth when one of Una's cloven hooves pressed against her knee.

Sid and Mateo exchanged a long look before getting into the front. Both deposited their sandwiches, beverages, and snacks into Mateo's lap as Sid took the wheel. Meanwhile, Alexa exhaled slowly through her nose and let her head fall against the seat's headrest. The monster hadn't come crashing down from the night sky, but its presence lingered behind her eyes.

There is something different about you. Una lifted its head, eyes shining from the blanket's shadowed folds. The wind sighed through the hole in the ceiling, and for the first time, Alexa wondered what they would do if it started to rain.

"I'm fine," Alexa said and turned to the window.

"Any music requests?" Mateo asked as he hooked his phone up to her sound system.

"Your choice." Alexa pressed her forehead to the cool glass.

"Seriously?" Mateo craned his neck to meet her eyes. "You sure?"

"Yeah. Play me something fun."

"You got it."

Mateo handed her a turkey and cheese sandwich. Unfortunately, Alexa's appetite disappeared the moment she walked into the bathroom. She turned the wrapped package over in her hands. She really ought to eat something. The salty reek of the turkey made her stomach turn in distaste. Maybe later.

The explosive 80s synth style of a Chappell Roan song overtook the speakers. Mateo smirked between bites of his sandwich, grooving in his seat. Sid put the car into the drive and bopped along to the beat, mouthing the lyrics,

For a sweet moment, Alexa enjoyed the goofy energy between the two boys as Mateo sang at the top of his lungs during the chorus. Alexa joined in, singing the words in Una's face.

Una snapped its teeth and drooped its ears. *I cannot wait to get off this planet.*

Chapter Twenty-One

THE INTERSTATE TURNED into an undulating black ribbon as they left Wyoming and entered Utah. At that point, Mateo whipped out a map of the United States and mentioned they only had one day left of driving before they ran into the ocean.

One more day? They all knew a lot could happen in a single day.

Alexa wished they weren't crossing the mountain range at night. Now that she wasn't driving, she fought to see where the mountains stopped and the sky began. The artist in her was sad to miss the opportunity to sketch the wild vistas hidden behind darkness.

Much to her relief, the monster remained quiet as the hour grew late. The invader coiled around the crown of her forehead, sinking its needle claws into the folds of her brain but halted further expansion. She pictured a cat made of black cloud curling into the tight space. She prodded the area with the tips of her fingers, wondering if she could feel any difference. All she touched was scratched skin.

Hours passed, and soon, a series of signs announced their arrival in Salt Lake City. Nearly a whole day had passed since they had gone through anything so big and bright. Nevertheless, Una was as bored as before, resting its beautiful head upon Alexa's lap. She tentatively laid a hand against the unicorn's cornsilk mane. Una didn't protest. The Bright One closed its blue eyes and dozed, enjoying Alexa's fingers through its hair.

Mountains receded as the traffic thickened. Alexa noted that the chain stores and restaurants are similar to those in and around the Twin Cities. The prettier parts of the city were tucked behind a warehouse district. They passed through in less than an hour. The city's glow gradually faded behind them.

Alexa grew sleepy, the excitement of seeing a new city waning. With her cozy sweatshirt and the weight of Una's head upon her lap, sleep tugged at her eyes. The monster's quiet presence made her wonder how such a massive being fit in her head. How many places could a single entity be at once? And why didn't it possess her like it had Debbie? Wouldn't Sid or Mateo be just as good of an option?

The unanswered questions continued to pile up as Una gently snored in her lap. Mateo had turned the pop music down to a dull roar. Sid and Mateo continue to bop their heads to another snappy song. Feeling safe and secure for the time being, Alexa let herself relax against the backseat.

Time extended and stretched, becoming a blackbird shaking out its wings and taking flight across the dark heavens. Alexa seemed to soar on the back of the bird, lifting on the mountain breeze. Then she became the bird momentarily before finding herself dangling from the raptor's talons. They flew over a lake of roiling black clouds, and the bird let her go.

She fell in the way one falls through dreams. Warm tendrils of clouds curled around her body. The sensation was pleasant at first, like walking through a lovely summer fog until the tendrils encased her arms and legs and spread across the rest of her body.

WE LET THIS GO ON FOR LONG ENOUGH, AND GROW WEARY OF YOUR INEPTITUDE.

The monster filled everything around her and shook her to her marrow. A flash of green swept through the void.

YOU MUST STOP RUNNING. TELL US WHERE YOU ARE OR WE WILL USE FORCE.

Alexa was no more than a leaf floating in a vast ocean. The warmth swelled, creeping near her mouth and nose, threatening to bury her alive. She flailed against the assault, but she couldn't move.

YOU DO NOT KNOW WHAT YOU ARE TRYING TO SAVE.

She gasped, finding the breath to say, "I won't let you hurt us."

YOU CANNOT STOP US.

"Get out of my head!" Alexa found a kernel of strength within her and held on tight. She had her own power, her own hidden courage. If she dug deep, she could push back and fight.

FOOLISH EARTH CREATURE. TELL US WHERE YOU ARE. ENOUGH OF THIS GAME.

"Go fuck yourself!"

Gathering every particle of strength within her being, Alexa shoved back. The monster roared, offended as she dared to sit up in the darkness. The warm fog receded, no longer wrapping her limbs. The bird of sleep returned, plucked her from the void and lifted her back into the waking world.

Covered in a film of sweat, Alexa woke in the back of the car, surrounded by frightened, shadowed faces. She pushed everyone away, leaned forward, and cradled her head in her hands. Every inch of her trembled. During her nightmare, she had soaked through her stocking cap and t-shirt.

"Lex, enough is enough. What the hell is going on?" Mateo grabbed her hand and forced her to look at him.

"Holy fucking shit, Lex. You were making the most awful sounds." Sid, still driving, watched Alexa from the rearview mirror.

Una pricked its ears forward and quietly studied her. *There is no need to hide anymore, Alexa Baxter. I am not the only one in your head.*

Alexa grasped Mateo's hand tight. "I don't know if I can explain it."

Yes, you can. Una snorted. The unicorn pressed its mole-soft muzzle against her damp brow and inhaled sharply. Una's whiskers scratched and poked her slick face as the Bright One sniffed every inch of her skull. The unicorn took a final, deep breath and drew back, baring its teeth. *There it is. I smell corruption, Alexa Baxter.*

Mateo waved a hand in Una's direction. "What's all that about? That's not a happy reaction, Lex."

Sid said, "Try to explain. We want to help you."

"Oh, God, it's so insane I can barely say it," Alexa sputtered, wiping away tears.

The details had already begun to fade. What once rang sharp and clear in her brain dulled. She couldn't recall the monster's exact words anymore, yet she knew what it wanted.

"Lex, you need to tell us," Mateo said.

"Okay, okay, okay." Alexa brushed back her damp hair and took a deep breath. "The monster isn't just chasing us. It's also in my head."

Silence followed her admission.

"In your *head?*" Mateo let go of her hand and stared at her wide-eyed. "But we haven't—how is that—it doesn't make any sense."

"I know, that sounds insane, right?" Alexa rubbed her temple and avoided Una's sharp gaze. "But, I can feel it. Like, clawing through my brain."

"*Clawing?*" Sid said. "How does that happen? Does it hurt?"

"Yeah, a lot," Alexa said and poked Una's nearest leg. "Please tell me you have an explanation."

Una snorted, flicked its ears, and trained its unblinking stare upon Alexa. *Perhaps I made a mistake by trying to communicate with you, Alexa Baxter.*

"Mistake?" Alexa ran her damp hand across her equally damp head and shivered. "Explain."

When I first encountered you, do you remember an odd sensation in your head?

Alexa remembered feeling overwhelmed when she met Una, a creature from a storybook trapped in the bathroom of her favorite park. Then she helped free the unicorn, and Una thanked her by slicing up her hands. Her still-aching hands. So much had happened at once. She had so many odd sensations she couldn't pick one.

"I guess?" Alexa said. "It was a lot to process at the time."

Una let out a sigh. *I surveyed you when I realized you were not a threat but a potential ally. I found your mind to be amenable to telepathic communication. I should have taken into consideration who else might discover this. But I had no choice. If you could not understand me, how could you ever help me?*

Alexa said, "If I'm hearing you right, because you can communicate with me, it means the monster can do it the same way you are?"

I never imagined such a thing could happen. Una shifted beside Alexa and drew its face closer to her. *Look at me. I need to take a closer look. And try not to blink.*

"Have I mentioned how much I hate it when you two do this?" Mateo folded his arms across his chest. "What are you talking about? You can talk to the monster, even when it's not here?"

"Yeah, an update would be nice." Sid snapped from the driver's seat.

Alexa blinked once, then held her eyes open as she continued to shiver. A feeling similar and yet different than the monster touched the front of her skull. The sensation was quite pleasant in comparison. Una's presence oozed around the itching place where the monster had taken root. The monster seemed to recognize what Una was doing and stabbed one of its paws deep into Alexa's brain.

Alexa whimpered and drew back. "What did you see?"

You are correct. The monster has inserted part of themselves into your mind. The unicorn made a series of angry snorts and shook its head. *I should have been more careful when I first probed you. I left a crack, and the monster took advantage of my mistake.*

"A crack?" Alexa yelped.

You must not let the monster overtake you, or we will all be doomed.

A whirling flicker of red and blue lights appeared out of the night behind them.

The confusion in the Civic went quiet once the teenagers realized a highway patrol car's flashing lights were heading their way. Silent, wide-eyed exchanged blinks between Alexa, Sid, and Mateo. Una immediately understood the lights and sirens were bad and asked Alexa to cover it up.

"Shit, shit, shit, what do I do?" Sid cried.

"We gotta pull over," Mateo said. He turned and squinted into the harsh lights. "We weren't speeding. Maybe we've got a taillight out. It'll be okay. We just need to stay calm."

"Calm?" Sid shrieked.

"Yes," Mateo said. "Don't act nervous, and keep your hands where the cop can see them."

Chapter Twenty-Two

SID HIT THE BRAKES while Alexa and Mateo stared into the headlight's glare.

"What are we going to do?" Sid squirmed behind the wheel. "I wasn't speeding. I was going the speed limit."

"Must be a taillight." Mateo's mouth formed a grim line. "They use that as an excuse to pull over my brothers all the time."

"Where did it even come from?" Alexa clutched her bandaged hands.

"Turn on your hazards," Mateo said, the calm in the storm.

Sid pulled onto the highway shoulder. "I don't know how."

Mateo leaned over and hit the hazard switch. "Keep your hands on the steering wheel as they approach and crack your window. I'll turn on the cab light."

"What? Why?" Sid did as Mateo directed and laid his trembling hands on the steering wheel.

"Mom went through all this with me when I was sixteen." Mateo switched on the overhead light. "We call it driving while brown. I'm surprised your parents didn't do the same."

"Please don't bring them up right now." Sid hissed.

They collectively held their breath as the patrolman hit the spotlight, flooding the cab in blazing white light. Alexa's heart thrashed in her chest. Hopefully, they would just get a ticket for whatever they had done wrong and be on their way.

"Don't move a muscle, Una," Alexa whispered.

Obviously, Alexa Baxter.

The spotlight-limned silhouette of an impressively built man approached the driver's side window. He knocked on the glass with the end of his flashlight. "Do you know how fast you were driving?"

"Uh, yes … sir." Sid stuttered, hands shaking despite resting on the steering wheel. "I had the cruise control at 70. That's the speed limit here, right?"

Alexa studied the cop's face hidden beneath the shadowed brim of his hat. Headlights gleamed off a curve of freshly shaved cheek.

"License and registration," the patrolman said in the calm, commanding tone of someone who knew the power of his authority. He shined his flashlight into the car, blinding each of them one by one.

"Ugh, it's in my back pocket." Sid slowly reached behind him. "Lex, where's your registration?"

"Glove compartment," Alexa said.

Mateo, his hands steady, opened the glove compartment and pulled out Alexa's registration. Sid handed the documentation to the shadow-faced officer. He took his time reviewing the documents. The wind whistled faintly through the hole in the ceiling, the mountain breeze playing a single long note.

Una was no more than a strange lump beside Alexa. All it would take was one shift, one deep exhale of breath, for the unicorn to become more than just a blanket.

"This car is registered to Alexa Baxter. Why are you driving it … Sidhit Dayani? Where is Alexa Baxter?"

"I'm here." Alexa squeaked from the back, raising her hand. She was blinded once again by the flashlight.

"Why are you not driving, Alexa Baxter?" The officer demanded, voice cold and monotonous.

"I, uh, was tired and thought it made more sense for Sid to drive."

The patrolman said, "What are you all doing out here in the middle of the night?"

"Visiting colleges." Mateo tried to smile, but it turned into a grimace

"And what is your destination?"

Alexa cleared her tight throat. "We're heading to California. First Berkley, then Stanford."

"Where in California?"

Alexa croaked, "I just said—"

"Please step out of the vehicle, Alexa Baxter." The patrolman took a step away from Sid and toward her.

"Step out?" Alexa said.

"Sir, I don't understand—" Sid began.

"Do I need to repeat myself?" The flashlight slashed from face to face, illuminating three sets of confused and frightened eyes.

Mateo murmured, "Alexa, maybe you shouldn't—"

"No, no, it's okay. I'll get out." Alexa pulled the door handle, took a deep breath, and took her time leaving the safety of her Civic. This all just had to be a misunderstanding. If she kept her wits about her, the patrolman would see nothing was amiss. They hadn't done anything illegal, as far as Alexa knew.

Alexa shivered as the mountain wind lashed against her. Her damp hair stuck to her scalp, and the cold seeped through her sweatshirt and into her soggy t-shirt. Man, she really needed a shower.

The patrol car's lights flashed a blue-and-red staccato against her weary eyes. No cars passed. They were deep in the middle of nowhere. The darkness of everything beyond both cars stood in stark contrast.

The officer loomed over Alexa, his face half-in shadow, his expression flat. She had to be at least a foot shorter than him. He directed her to stand next to her trunk, facing him.

"What is your destination?" He repeated, his voice empty of all emotion.

"I said California? We're visiting colleges?" The lights were too much to handle. She shaded her eyes.

"Hands at your side, Alexa Baxter."

"Tell me exactly where in California."

Alexa's throat tightened. "Well, UC Berkeley is in, um, Berkeley?"

"YOU ARE LYING TO US." The patrolman approached and stood so close Alexa couldn't help but back into her trunk.

The wind blew her damp hair, and a chill settled deep in her bones. Her teeth chattered as she said, "S-sir, if we've done something wrong—"

"WHERE ARE YOU GOING?"

"Berkeley?"

"LIAR. WHERE ARE YOU GOING?" The officer towered over her. His voice was flat in a familiar way. Flat like Debbie when she shoved her against the wall. Flat like the voice thundering in her dreams.

"If you want Una so much, why don't you just pull it out of the car?" Alexa squared her shoulders and glared up at the monster.

A meaty hand reached out and took her by the throat. Voices shouted from inside the car. Alexa slumped against her trunk, fingers grasping at the officer's hand. He wasn't constricting her breathing. The gesture was meant to frighten her. Well, it was working.

"WHERE ARE YOU GOING?"

"I don't know. We don't know," Alexa gasped into the hard lines of the face above hers.

"STOP LYING TO US OR WE WILL HURT YOU."

A flash of light bounced and shattered beside them. The monster pivoted, taking Alexa with him; no more than a rag doll in his clutches, the monster swung her through the air while both hands grasped her neck. She tried to scream, but the sound came out in a raspy squeak. Breathing grew difficult. Dark spots clouded her vision. At the same time, a bang and a squeal of metal exploded a few feet to her right.

Straining, Alexa discovered Una bucking and kicking where the monster had stood seconds before. The unicorn let out a horrible cry. Una had shoved its horn into Alexa's trunk when attempting to disembowel the officer. The Bright One was stuck. The monster barked out an empty laugh and tossed Alexa to the ground. She fell to her knees, scraping against the gravel beneath her feet.

Mateo appeared behind her, helping her back off the ground. His eyes shone in horror at the scene beyond Alexa. "Holy shit, Lex. Are you okay?"

Before she could respond, the ham-sized hands of the patrolman grasped Alexa's shoulders. Mateo held on to the hem of her sweatshirt as the monster-officer dragged Alexa toward the patrol car.

Sid had joined the fray, trying to free Una from the trunk. Una made the situation worse, kicking and bucking at Sid.

Alexa had never been subject to physical cruelty before. Her body shook, both rigid and limp at the same time. She could do little more than push uselessly at the giant hands dragging her across the asphalt. Mateo, arms spread wide and pleading, followed in the wake of Alexa and the monster while Sid continued to deal with Una.

Una's voice railed in Alexa's head in an incomprehensible tirade of rage. The monster tossed Alexa onto the patrol car's hood, knocking the air from her lungs. She writhed on the car hood, struggling for breath.

ENOUGH OF THIS. TELL US WHERE YOU ARE GOING. The monster thundered as he pressed her shoulders into the car hood. Metal buckled beneath her.

"I don't know!" Alexa cried.

The lantern-jawed face of the possessed officer contorted in rage above her, pounding his fists into the car hood.

"Stop, stop, please stop hurting her." Mateo cowered in the officer's shadow, reaching for Alexa but afraid to touch the patrolman.

"Monster! It's the monster," Alexa said. A ragged scream curdled in her throat as the monster grabbed her off the hood. The world spun. Would it try to kill her?

"TELL US!" The monster roared into Alexa's face. The sound ripped raw and terrible through the officer's throat, and spittle hit her cheeks.

When she had no answer, the monster tossed her into the ditch. She hit the hard earth on her side. Every part of her cried out in painful protest. Mateo shrieked and shoved at the monster. The possessed man lurched after Mateo and swatted him away like a fly.

The screech of bending metal and a flash of white announced that Una had wretched itself free from the trunk. Una charged the monster, horn a gleaming lance. The monster dodged the onslaught just in time, and Una sprawled into the middle of the highway.

Everything hurt as Alexa pushed herself to her knees. The patrol lights whirled, her friends shouted, the monster officer growled, and Una struggled to find footing. Una's rage resounded through her brain.

"Oh my God, oh my God, oh my God." Mateo scrambled back to Alexa when the officer's attention turned to Una. "This is fucking insane."

Alexa clutched her throbbing head. "The monster is in the cop. And Una—oh, God, we can't let Una hurt him!"

Chapter Twenty-Three

THE MONSTER CANNOT take me in this false form. Una leaped to its feet.

In the pulsating lights of the patrol car, Una seemed to expand. Sinew and muscle stretched taught against its radiant hide. The brilliant creature brandished its horn, slashing it against the dark. Steam rose from Una's flared nostrils, and the once delicate beast became genuinely terrifying.

"YOU CAN RUN ALL YOU WANT, BRIGHT ONE," the monster thundered. "WE WILL FIND YOU. AS FAR AND FAST AS YOU RUN, WE WILL FIND YOU."

Not if I kill you first.

Una charged. The possessed officer laughed. Alexa screamed, "Una, no! Don't hurt him."

Sid awakened and hurled his body at Una as the unicorn passed him, shoving it off-course. His explosion of force startled Alexa. She had forgotten Sid was a varsity athlete.

Una skittered into the gravel, and the monster bellowed, "IMBECILES EACH ANY EVERY ONE OF YOU. THIS HUMAN BODY MAY BE WEAK BUT YOU ALL KNOW THE POWER OF OUR GATHERED FORM."

The unicorn reeled and recovered its footing in a flash. Una flicked its lion tail, rounded its shoulders, and again charged the monster.

"Una, no! Don't hurt him!" Alexa pushed herself to her feet.

Sid, assisted by the monster, shoved Una away as it charged, but not in time to stop the unicorn from taking a small piece of Sid with it. Sid gasped and grabbed his side. The monster heaved Sid away from him and continued to laugh its awful, gargled chortle. Una skidded to a stop in the center of the highway, dazzling and terrible.

"Una! That's enough, goddamn it!" Alexa waved her arms and scrambled up the embankment, Mateo at her heels. "If you hurt that cop, we're all fucked."

Sid leaned against the side of the Civic, clutching his side.

A thousand horrifying scenarios raced through Alexa's mind. "Sid?"

Sid lifted his shirt to examine the wound. A thin red line marred his perfect torso.

"It's not deep," Sid said as blood oozed to the surface. He winced as she prodded the cut running from his navel to the base of his ribs. "Just a bad scratch."

"Shit," Alexa spat. If the unicorn had been only an inch closer when it cut him, they would be begging the patrolman to take Sid to the nearest emergency room. Una could have disemboweled him. Alexa wished to wrap her arms around Sid. Instead, she settled for grasping his arm.

I have journeyed too far for this to end now. Una snorted and paced along the circle of headlights, eyes gleaming wild and murderous.

"If you hurt him, we'll never get to the Rift," Mateo said, wrapping a protective arm around Alexa. He leaned close and whispered, "We should just hop in the car and run."

"Best idea I heard all day." Sid's eyes fixed upon the two deadly beasts staring each other down.

"Una, please," Alexa said. "Get back in the car. Let's just go."

And just keep running? Forever? Una raged silently, whipping its tail, hooves clicking across the empty road.

"What other choice do we have?" Alexa said. "That's only part of the monster. The part in me is no different. Would you hurt me too?"

Una turned away from the monster and lowered its head. *I would not hurt you, Alexa Baxter. I would never hurt you.*

A wicked grin spread across the officer's borrowed face. THIS IS FAR FROM OVER. UNTIL NEXT TIME.

The patrolman's slackened. He fell back against the squad car and slid toward the road. In a moment, he appeared utterly unconscious.

"Until next time." Alexa dropped to a crouch, relieved and wrung out from the attack. The monster was right. Everything was so far from over.

Una's horn slashed the air as the unicorn whinnied and tossed its head. The Bright One approached the slumped man and sniffed the officer while the humans held their collective breath. The unicorn snorted, blew upon the officer's slack face, and returned to the Civic.

We need to go. Una stood at the back door and glowered at the three humans. The Bright One was once again just a unicorn. The blazing power that had seethed from every limb had left as quickly as it arrived.

"Can we leave? Is it over?" Sid asked. He twisted up the front of his shirt and assessed his injury.

"I guess?" Mateo blinked into the flickering lights.

Sid said, "Lex?"

Every part of her ached, from her head to her feet. Her crouched position wasn't comfortable, but if she got up too fast, she might puke. She touched her neck, sensing the bruises blossoming beneath her skin. The bandages on her hands protected them from further injury while the monster tossed her around, but the edges were a dirty, frayed mess.

Alexa wanted to cry, scream, collapse on the road, and let the dark sky spin above her. She looked back at the highway patrolman and noticed him twitch.

"He's waking up." Mateo took her arm and helped her stand. "We gotta go."

The world swum before her eyes; her stomach churned.

"How many fingers am I holding up?" Mateo waved his hands in front of her.

"Four?" Alexa coughed.

"Works for me." Mateo put an arm under hers and helped her toward the backseat.

"Should we leave him like that?" Alexa pointed to the officer, who started groaning and moving his legs. "What if he was wearing a camera? Or what about a dash cam? He's not going to understand."

"What do you think he'd see if anything recorded what just happened?" Mateo placed his hands on either side of her face so she had to look directly into his frightened eyes.

"I don't know," Alexa said.

Sid had already returned to the driver's seat while Una climbed into the back and muttered impatient words in her head. She rubbed her skull, wishing all invaders would cease and desist for a few moments so she could collect her thoughts.

"They will see a police officer assaulting a girl half his size." Mateo guided her to the open back door. "And then they'll see some shit no one will ever believe."

"Yeah, I suppose." Alexa let Mateo help her into the back seat.

"Holy shit, that was insane." Mateo clicked Alexa's seatbelt into place and let out a long breath.

"I know," Alexa said as Mateo shut her door. Una curled up beside her, looking up at Alexa with its galaxy eyes. Eyes that minutes before were those of a dangerous, murderous beat. "So many monsters."

Chapter Twenty-Four

A NEW MONSTER HAD REVEALED itself and sat at Alexa's side. The girl and the unicorn contemplated each other. Una stared, unblinking at Alexa, and Alexa returned the stare. She monitored the unicorn's every move. Alexa had underestimated the Bright One. Violence was hidden in a pretty package.

Mateo turned into a mother hen as they continued down the dark highway—a stream of questions and concerns issued from his lips while he monitored his battered friend. Alexa, dull from the exhaustion of the whole incident, promised Mateo if she needed anything, she would let him know.

Sid drove like a man in shock. His eyes appeared to lose focus from moment to moment. More than once, he rubbed his eyes and sent the car weaving into the other lane. The third time it happened, Mateo was so freaked out he offered to finally take his turn driving. Sid refused, gripping the steering wheel like a lifeline.

Battered and bruised, Alexa tried to find a comfortable position in the back seat. She arranged and rearranged Una's legs over her lap. For once, Una didn't complain. The unicorn's hard eyes softened with each small cry of pain from Alexa.

You are very hurt, Alexa Baxter. Una sniffed her.

"I guess that's what happens after a monster throws you around like a rag doll," Alexa said.

Will you be all right? Una's whiskers tickled her cheek as it sniffed her neck. *You do not appear to be bleeding, but I can smell the pain beneath your skin. I need you to stay strong, Alexa Baxter. Now more than ever.*

Alexa frowned. "You know, you can't go around attacking people possessed by the monster. It wasn't the cop's fault. He couldn't control himself."

How can you say that after what they did to you?

"I need you to promise never to charge anyone else." Alexa shook her finger in Una's face. "No matter what."

If I had not charged the monster, they might have killed you.

"You don't know that." Alexa groaned and attempted one more rearrangement of her limbs. She brushed at a clod of dirt sticking to her sweatshirt. What she wouldn't give for a bath.

Mateo ignored the one-sided conversation and put on a little music. A gentle, love-torn ballad wove through the Civic. Sid began drifting toward the left. Instead of screeching a warning, Mateo rested his hands on the steering wheel and helped correct his direction. Sid flinched, sat up straighter, and thanked Mateo for his help.

Never dismiss the monster's power; they will consume you from the inside out. Never doubt that they will do whatever it takes to get to me. To us. Getting off this planet is vital to our survival.

"Well, I'm sure trying." Alexa held up her bandaged hands.

I know. I am sorry for your pain. I need you. I cannot get off this damned planet without you. But I will not let anything stop me.

Alexa spoke low enough that Sid and Mateo couldn't hear her. "Promise if the monster somehow gets in Mateo or Sid, you won't hurt them."

As long as they do not get in the way.

Alexa poked the unicorn's muzzle. "Promise."

I do not make—

"Una. Promise."

Una snorted and laid back its ears. *I will not hurt them.*

"That's better." Alexa turned her tired face to the window and pressed her bruised cheeks against the cool glass.

The night drew out dark and unending. The change of energy within the car had a taste to it. Bitter. Cold. Little steel between the teeth. Everyone was awake, staring out their window, weary and blinking in the dead of night. Too tired to speak and too shaken to sleep.

Despite everything, Alexa couldn't help but close her eyes. She shook awake a moment later when a light jab poked her forearm. She recoiled when she realized Una had poked her with its horn.

You cannot sleep, Alexa Baxter.

Alexa rubbed the place where Una poked her. "What are you talking about?"

The crack I left in your brain makes you vulnerable when you sleep. The monster will try to overtake you again. They will try to trick you into telling them where we are.

"Why does the monster need to know where we are? Can't it just use my eyes or the eyes of someone else it possesses?"

That is not how this works. Mental projection is complicated. They may see a sign but do not know what it means, just as I see many signs and have no idea what they say. I cannot read them. But a name. A name can be found and translated.

"Then how does the monster manage to possess people close to us? And can't they use the possessed person's brain to translate the signs?"

The monster can locate your mental signature and the signatures of those near you. Now that your brain is corrupted, they can monitor your location somewhat. However, we are moving too fast for them in the physical plane. Moving through the fourth dimension is quite different from the third.

"Fourth dimension?" Alexa said. It sounded like some New Age stuff her funky aunt spouted at Thanksgiving. "So, let's make this clear. If I say our location, the monster can find it. But it doesn't know English?"

And there are things I do not understand about the monster either. They are wise to keep all their tricks to themselves. And, no offense, some of this is simply too complicated for a simple Earth creature.

"There you go again," Alexa said. "Underestimating me and my friends."

Una snorted and laid back its ears. *I have underestimated the monster, which was foolish of me. They are clever in ways I never predicted.*

"They, you keep saying 'they.' So, there must be more than one monster after us."

As you can see and feel right now, the monster is made of many parts. They can be a large and powerful collective whole or divide themselves into smaller but weaker bits. Keeping them in many places at once is ideal. They can only truly harm us if they come together as a whole. And they still do not know where we are going.

"What great news." The urge to scratch at her forehead returned, prickling and insistent. She pressed her thumb into the biggest cut on her palm to redirect the pain. "Any idea how much farther?"

We grow closer with each mile. The Rift is calling to me in a more unmistakable voice than before.

"There's a rest area up ahead." Sid's voice broke through their conversation. "I need a break."

Alexa startled. She had forgotten that the world didn't revolve around her and Una for a moment.

"And I need to pee." Mateo unwound his limbs from the ball he had formed in the passenger seat.

A sign for Pequot Summit Rest Area flashed by. Sid didn't wait for permission to pull over. The dashboard clock read four in the morning. The mountainous world remained hidden in the dark, and the road was empty.

The rest area consisted of a parking lot and a simple wood building with two doors: one for the men's room and one for the women's. Concrete highway barriers surrounded the structure, likely keeping it from being plowed over in the deep winter.

Is this necessary? Una snorted and knocked the tip of its horn against the glass in an irritated rhythm.

"Mateo needs to pee. Sid needs a break." Alexa opened her door the moment Sid parked the car. She gingerly stepped out of the vehicle, each joint and muscle protesting. After she let out a whimper, Mateo hurried to her side to help her limp across the parking lot.

Alexa knew the real reason they stopped. The three of them needed to talk, assess the situation, and decide what to do next. Unfortunately, Una leaped out of the car behind Alexa, a delicate beacon glimmering in the darkness. Above them, the stars shone bright. Alexa gave herself a moment to appreciate the view of the sky without a kindle of light pollution.

A pop of light broke Alexa's reverie. Sid had switched on the flashlight on his phone and played it over the rocky ground.

"Let's just all use the same bathroom. Safety in numbers," Mateo said.

"Yeah, makes sense." Alexa picked up what he was putting down.

Make it quick, Alexa Baxter. I will stretch my legs, and we shall continue. No more stops until the sun rises.

Chapter Twenty-Five

NONE OF THEM WERE DRESSED warm enough for the weather. The three teenagers clustered shoulder to shoulder as they followed Sid's flashlight to the nearest bathroom. Una hovered on the periphery, pacing the edge of the parking lot. They hadn't seen a vehicle's headlights or tail lights in hours, not since the highway patrol car materialized out of the darkness.

The cold oozed through Alexa's clothes. She wrapped her arms around her waist, and a whoosh of body odor puffed through her collar. She sighed in half-hearted disgust and wished again for a bath.

Mateo yanked open the steel door, hinges grinding from lack of use, and they stepped into the women's bathroom. Sid found a light switch, and a weak, yellow glow lit the space. Silent at first, they blinked at each other. Each appeared in various states of shock.

Alexa went to the nearest mirror to survey her injuries. Finger-shaped bruises covered her throat, and when she poked them, a deep pain sunk along her neck. She brushed at the patch of dirt clinging to her elbows and knees, sensing other bruises beneath the fabric.

"No offense, but you look like shit, Lex." Mateo surveyed his friend. "We really should get you to a hospital."

Alexa shook her head. "You know we can't."

"What if you have internal bleeding?" Mateo looked closer at her neck.

"I don't think I do," Alexa said.

Sid did something completely unexpected. He carefully gathered Alexa's broken body into his strong arms. They hissed in pain at the same time when he pressed Alexa to him.

"What about you?" Alexa drew back.

Sid lifted his shirt—she would never get tired of him doing that—and examined the red slash along his lower torso. A scab had formed, and the wound was no longer bleeding, nor did it look infected.

"It's just a scratch." Sid poked the cut and dropped his shirt. "In another world, I would have fucked up Una for this."

Alexa murmured, "Una is much more dangerous than I realized."

"I don't care," Sid grumbled, eyes defiant.

Mateo grasped each of them by the shoulders and gestured for them to gather closer. He whispered, "We need to get away from it."

Sid nodded. "Absolutely."

A cold thread of fear pricked Alexa's chest. "How can we?"

"We could rush the car right now and leave it out here," Mateo said.

"It's too fast." Sid's eyes traced something on Alexa's face. "Didn't you see how fast it moved? I barely deflected Una away from the cop."

"Staying alive is our priority," Alexa said, running a hand through her dusty scalp. "This won't be over until we get Una to the Rift. From the sound of it, we should be close. I'm sure we can hang on one more day."

Mateo folded one of Alexa's wrecked hands into his own. "At what cost? I watched that monster throw you through the air, Lex. You could have died. I don't want any of us to die."

"What if we just walked?" Sid said. "Walked away until someone found us."

Alexa backed a step. They didn't understand the total weight of everything. They didn't know they were on the losing side of all this. One step in the wrong direction and Alexa could fall.

"Una will never let us walk away." Alexa pressed a hand to the back of her neck and discovered additional bruises. "Remember what it tried to do to the cop? Una is incredibly dangerous, maybe as dangerous as the monster. Anyway, I couldn't walk a mile like this. I hurt everywhere."

"Shouldn't we try?" Mateo begged.

"You have no idea." Alexa blinked back tears. "The monster is in my brain, sort of like Una but in a different, scarier way. How can I get away from anything if they're in my head? I'm too tired to run. Neither of them would let me go without a fight."

Hot tears grew cold as they ran down her dirty cheeks. Alexa turned to the sink to hide her distress and switched on the faucet. The water bit into her hands but felt wonderful against her aching face. The bandages on her hands wrinkled and sagged.

Stupid bandages. Stupid bruises. Stupid monster tiptoeing along the crown of her head. In a frenzy, she ripped and pulled at the soaked bandages, tossing them to the floor. She plunged her hands under the cold water and picked out a piece of gravel from the heel of her hand.

Sid reached out to Alexa, resting his hand on her shoulder. Another hand pressed against her right shoulder: Mateo. The tears dribbled down her face with the cold water, indistinguishable from one another. The bathroom didn't have paper towels, and when she knocked at the hand dryer, a stream of air blew more tepidly than hot.

"If we get Una where it needs to go, then all this will be over." She turned to meet the boys' eyes. "We have no choice. I'll drive there myself if I have to. Una won't let me sleep anyway."

A loud bang shook the bathroom door. The three humans jumped, still grasping each other.

What is going on in there? Are you finished?

Alexa unsteadily shouted, "Just peeing!"

I hear you all whispering, Alexa Baxter.

"Almost done!" Alexa said in a too cheerful voice. "Look, we must have one more day of driving before we hit the ocean. I think I can hang on if you two support me. I just want this to end. I want them both out of my head."

"This is insane." Mateo gave a resigned sigh.

They flinched as the unicorn banged against the door yet again. *Finish up now. We must go. We cannot waste any more time.*

"Just a second!" Alexa said. "I need you to promise to help Una get to wherever it's going. Then that'll be over. We can go home and try to sort out our lives."

"Okay." Sid nodded, standing a little straighter. "I'll drive as far as I can, then you're up, Mateo."

Alexa turned to her dearest friend. "Mateo?"

"Yeah, let's do this." Mateo nodded, lips pressed tight. "Let's get this thing home."

Chapter Twenty-Six

AS THE SUN ROSE ON the third day of their unexpected journey across the American West, Alexa's Civic rumbled down the dusty expanse of upper Nevada. The world was a quilt of textured browns alternating from russet to umber, then ocher and back again. Hills rose in the distance, and the shadows of mountains hung near the horizon.

Mateo scanned his phone to see if there was any news about their encounter with the highway patrolman. Nothing had come up so far and they had a feeling nothing would. How would the officer react to finding himself where he shouldn't be? Would he have any memory of what happened or what he had done?

Under the sunrise's buttery light, Alexa found more bruises on her arms and holes in her jeans. Her knees were especially sore, and her right ankle had swollen overnight, but not too bad. Each new bruise brought with it the memory of the giant man's hands around her throat. She dealt with the trickle of violence-laced images from her Civic's backseat by focusing on the landscape. In her heart, she knew she would never be the same after this terrible journey.

Several things became apparent in the light of day. First, Sid had to take a break from driving. They stopped in a town named Elko, and Mateo took over. After spending five minutes checking mirrors, he gripped the steering wheel and turned back onto the highway. Sid encouraged him at each mile marker.

Sid was half-delirious with exhaustion as he settled into the passenger seat. He turned back to Alexa, and from the tight knit of his brow, it was clear Alexa must look awful.

He stuck his fingers through the gap below the headrest and said, "You don't look so bad."

"Ha, don't lie." Alexa grinned and swiped a bead of sweat trickling down her forehead.

Alexa's internal temperature had gone haywire when the sun broke across the horizon. She had already sweat through her Nirvana t-shirt and couldn't stand wearing her stocking cap a second longer. She used the sweatshirt from the truck stop to mop away sweat dripping down the back of her neck. The only good part of the fever was that it deadened her aching body.

"I hope we find your Rift soon." Alexa threw back a mouthful of water from the stash they purchased in Elko.

Una blinked its big eyes and placed its head in her lap. *I sense we shall get there by the end of this day.* Una closed its eyes and let out a sigh.

"Good." Alexa swallowed another gulp of water.

"What did it say?" Sid glared at the unicorn with open disgust.

"This'll be over by the end of the day," she said.

"Finally, some good news." Mateo squeaked as a car passed them.

"How do we go home after all this?" Sid rested his brow against the headrest, eyes drooping half-closed.

"Let's worry about that tomorrow." Mateo's knuckles turned white, gripping the steering wheel as if his life depended upon it. His narrow shoulders rounded forward, and he hunched like an old man over the steering wheel.

"I have no idea how to go home after this," Alexa said. She started sipping her water, then realized she ought to ration each drop of water if it was going to last until they needed to refill the gas tank. The fewer times they stopped, the better.

"When I get home," Sid said, "I'm going to be nicer to my little sister."

"When I get home, I'm going to sleep for a week." Alexa brushed the sweat off her brow. "What about you, Mateo?"

"I want to shower so long the water turns cold," Mateo said. "I can't wait to sleep in my bed again. Eat my mom's amazing cooking. Pretend this never happened."

Sid yawned. "Sounds great."

Alexa winced as the monster's claws teased the space behind her eyes. Unseen spikes prodded the soft tissue. What were they looking for now? Weakness? Outside her window, strange shapes materialized in the sky. A curious, looping shadow embroidered the ice-blue heavens. Tendrils of grey unwound and blended into the clouds.

"Well, that's fun." She closed her eyes and massaged her lids. Tired in a way she never imagined she could be, she fought the lure of sleep. Instead, she opened her gluey eyelids and watched the monster's bizarre display in the sky.

Sid quickly succumbed to his need for rest. He curled against the seat, and his breath soon fell into a deep, steady rhythm.

"Will you ever tell him?" Mateo said after a few minutes.

Alexa sighed. "Probably not."

Mateo pouted at her in the rearview mirror. "This is your best chance. You've pined over him for as long as I've known you. What's the harm in finally admitting your feelings?"

"Because if I tell him, then my fantasy ends." Alexa pressed her hot forehead to the cool window. "I spent almost hours, sometimes, imagining the scenarios where he suddenly realizes how fascinating I am."

A lock of his dark hair strayed through the space beneath the headrest. Alexa touched a strand with quivering fingers.

Alexa said, "I like to imagine what it would be like to hold hands. Go out to a movie together. Kiss him. I'm not ready to lose that."

"Lex, come on. Really? I mean, think about all the shit we've gone through. Hell, you got beat up by a freakin' cop. Who knows what might happen today? This might be your last chance."

Their eyes met in the rearview mirror. Alexa said, "What if I tell him and he feels different? I can't add that to my crazy. Anyway, it's senior year. Soon, he'll head off to Harvard, or whatever, and we'll end up in the Cities, just like we planned."

"If we live through this."

"We're going to live through this," Alexa said with grim certainty. She would do anything for Mateo and now for Sid. She would do whatever it took to keep them alive, even at her own expense. She exhaled hard when she realized this truth.

"Are we?" Mateo said.

"I promise."

"Don't make promises you can't keep."

Alexa didn't answer.

Mateo said, "I'm with you. I won't let anything get in the way of us living our lives the way we want to. You'll always be my sister from another mister."

"You'll always be my number one." Alexa smiled.

"Besties forever?"

"Forever. No matter what."

Chapter Twenty-Seven

THE DAY DIDN'T IMPROVE for Alexa.

As they passed town after town, mile marker after mile marker, sign after sign telling them of the fascinating places they couldn't stop to appreciate, the monster dug deeper into her brain. However, Una's mood improved the further they went to the point that its voice actually sang in Alexa's head.

They reached Winnemucca, Nevada, after Una directed them to take an exit off the long-used Interstate 80. They stopped for fuel at a tidy but wilted gas station. Sid and Mateo followed the same routine they had fallen into along the way. Alexa wanted to get out and take in some fresh air, but she couldn't stand the idea of anyone seeing her in her ruined state. And worse, she wasn't sure her legs would still work without help from Sid or Mateo. That would definitely draw attention.

Sid opened her door and crouched in front of her. "Hey, kid."

"Can you get me some water, please?" she croaked.

Days before, sitting close to Sid would have made her wild with embarrassment, but now, seat-soaked and half-mad, she managed to force a smile.

Mateo stood near Sid as he pumped gas into the car. "I'm really worried about Lex. You're getting worse."

Sid took Alexa's hands and frowned. "Gosh, they're cold."

"I don't feel cold." Alexa tried to be brave. She folded into a lopsided lump. "Could you get me more water? Maybe a new shirt or a towel or something. God, I must reek."

"Nah, you smell great." Sid gave her hand a careful, reassuring squeeze. He brushed back the damp hair from her forehead in a startlingly intimate gesture. He leaned in and whispered into her ear, "I'm calling my parents when we get in the station. We can't watch you suffer like this any longer."

Alarmed, Alexa gripped Sid's hand with all her strength. "No, don't. Keep them out of it. They won't understand. And Una—I don't know what it will do."

Sid leaned in further, his face inches from hers. Despite being half-possessed by a monster, Alexa's heart fluttered in response. He was so beautiful. So perfect. With her free hand, she rested her fingers against his cheek. He didn't pull back, instead a smile flitted across his lips. He appeared to understand her without needing to say the words.

Sid said, "This is for the best. You're sick and hurt, Lex. And you need to get help."

Strange shadows tumbled through the air behind him. Impossible things etched across the sky. Freezing and yet boiling, she shuddered.

"After I make this call, I'm finding a hospital. Enough is enough." Sid rose from his crouch before she had the chance to respond and headed toward the gas station.

Alexa turned to the unicorn beside her. Una hadn't moved. Did the Bright One hear their conversation?

Alexa held her breath and considered the idea of abandoning the creature beside her. Was that the right choice? After everything that had happened? Maybe Sid was right. She had promised Una one more day but questioned if she had the strength to do it.

A more important question remained: Would Una *let* them leave it behind?

Una stirred and nudged a hoof against her thigh. *Have we stopped?*

"Just to get gas." Alexa lied.

Very well. This will be over soon, Alexa. I can feel it in my bones.

Alexa didn't turn away from the window. Her feelings for Una tangled in a whirl of anger and regret. She shouldn't have gone into the women's bathroom in Birkmose Park. She should have been smart and called animal control and let them deal with the otherworldly creature within.

As the monster picked at her brain and manipulated her body, the temptation to exchange one monster for another hung at the tip of her tongue. All she had to do was speak a few words, and the monster in her brain would hear. And then? Could it all be so simple? Just a couple of words?

"This better end soon." Alexa observed the ordinary people moving in and around the gas station. People going through another ordinary day, never knowing what was hidden on the other side of a door.

We will reach the Rift today. I can feel it, Alexa Baxter. Like the multiverse's currents racing through my veins. But we still have miles to go. I need you, Sid, and Mateo, to help me escape this world. You do not know what the monster will do to me. To us. You do not know what they have done to so many of my people. You know the word genocide, Alexa Baxter?

"Yes," Alexa whispered and half-closed her eyes. Despite Una's words, the urge to let the monster's weight collapse fully against her hummed at the tip of her tongue.

In the convenience store's windows, Sid paced circles. She placed a hand on her cheek, which he touched a moment before. Should she tell him how she felt? A ridiculous thought considering what sat within and beside her.

Sid's conversation animated his face. He stopped and broke into a smile. A look of relief filled his eyes. Alexa turned away. The relief was false. Temporary. If they headed toward a hospital, then what? Una wouldn't let them. Not for a second.

Sid and Mateo left the gas station, supplies in hand, a new black sweatshirt tucked in the crook of Sid's arm. The two boys beamed at each other. They were so full of hope that Alexa knew it couldn't last. Mateo opened the passenger door and handed Alexa one of three enormous bottles of water. He tossed her a wink and dropped into his seat. Alexa said nothing, her chest tight. What would Una do when they pulled up to a hospital instead of taking the nearest onramp?

"Everyone have their seatbelts on?" Sid adjusted a new pair of cheap sunglasses and started the car.

Alexa took a big gulp of water, attempting to cool the monster sitting within her. The fever had broken while the boys were in the gas station. Instead of relief, the change in temperature worried her. Something important had changed. Did the monster hear Sid's conversation?

"Hey, Lex, maybe a little walk might do you some good?" Sid said as they paused at a stoplight. He nodded to the cemetery across the street.

The last thing Alexa wanted to do was stroll through another cemetery, but some fresh air might be nice.

"What do you think, Lex?" Mateo turned back to Alexa, his eyes flickering between Sid and Alexa.

Alexa stretched her legs. They seemed more stable than twenty minutes ago. "Sure?"

Sid must have decided to let her in on the plan. From the slight nod of Mateo's head, he appeared to agree. Maybe if she could walk on her own, the boys would change their minds and continue heading West.

They pulled into the cemetery. Una stirred. A sliver of blue eye glistened through a part in the blanket. *What is going on? Why are we stopping again?*

"I just want to stretch my legs quick without anyone staring at me," Alexa reassured Una. "For a few minutes. I think I feel a little better, and a quick walk might help."

Five minutes at most?

"Sure, you got it," Alexa said.

Una snorted with displeasure. *Very well. Five minutes.*

The Winnemucca Cemetery was very different from the one in Wyoming. Though lined with trees and full of graves, half the cemetery grounds were covered with pavement or cement.

Sid parked, asked Mateo if he could "hold down the fort," and hopped out of the car. Mateo bobbed his head and relaxed back into his seat. Sid rounded the front of the Civic, opened Alexa's door, and held out his hand. With his help, getting out of the seat was easier than Alexa had anticipated.

She wobbled a moment. Sid wrapped an arm beneath her arms and said, "Careful. One step at a time." He closed the door behind them, and they set out through a row of gravestones.

Una's horn tapped on the window.

"Five minutes, I know." Sid gave Una the middle finger.

"Sid," Alexa giggled and swatted his hand.

Sid held her tighter. "Not like the alien knows what it means anyway."

Alexa let out a pure, honest laugh. Step after step, she gained confidence in her ability to walk. She could have asked Sid to pull away, but why would she do something so silly? For a moment, she walked in a dream, the boy she adored holding her tight to his chest.

"See, I don't need to go to the hospital," Alexa said once they rounded the first row of concrete-covered graves. "I'm feeling a lot better."

"Barely." Sid gave her a crooked grin and squeezed her hand.

"No, wait, watch." Alexa stepped out of his grasp and took a few precarious steps. "So much better. I can do this. Una says we're close, so let's keep going. We don't know what'll happen if we stop."

"Lex?" Sid paused. Alexa stared at her distorted reflection in his cheap aviator sunglasses.

Alexa's mouth went dry. "Yeah?"

"Can you answer a question for me?" He tugged her closer, his hands warm and snug around her cold fingers.

Her heart boomed in her chest. "Sure?"

"Are you telling us everything about Una? The whole truth?"

Alexa blinked, confused. "What do you mean?"

Sid put his hand against her hot cheek. His breath smelled of mint. "Has Una told us where we're going?"

"Sid, no, I don't—"

"You can tell me." Sid jerked back, his face contorting into a grimace. He pressed a hand against his head and moaned. With the other hand, he grasped Alexa too hard. "The Bright One must have told you where we are going."

"You know what I know," Alexa reassured him. The monster shivered beneath her forehead. "Hey, I think our five minutes are up. Let's get going."

"No." Sid grabbed Alexa's face. "YOU KNOW SOMETHING. WE DO NOT BELIEVE YOU."

His fingers pressed painfully into her skin. "Sid, you're hurting me."

Mateo jumped out of the car, slamming the door behind him. "Hey, what the hell are you doing, Sid?"

Sid convulsed. His grip on Alexa loosened. Alexa twisted away and held up a hand to Mateo, who was charging across the cemetery. Beyond him, the Honda rocked. Una must have seen the change in Sid too.

The unicorn thrashed in the back seat and silently screamed, *They are here. We must go. Leave the stupid boy behind.*

"Sid." Alexa turned to the boy she adored. "You can fight back. Push them down or away. You're stronger than them. You can do this."

Unlike Debbie or the patrolman, Sid understood what was happening to him.

"YOU WRETCHED EARTH CREATURE," Sid growled. The sunglasses fell from his face to reveal shining, obsidian eyes. "WE WILL DESTROY YOU ALL FOR THIS."

"I told you, we don't know where we're going," Alexa said, surprised to be so calm. She had to be the voice at the end of the tunnel calling Sid home. "This body-snatched thing you're trying to do won't work. You know that. Let him go. You're wasting everyone's time."

"IF THAT IS WHAT YOU WANT." Sid raised his black eyes to Alexa, an awful smirk disfiguring his face,

A twinge prickled at the base of her skull in addition to the ache beneath her forehead. At first, the change was similar to what she had experienced before until the monster's talons sunk into her brain, deeper and more painful than ever before. Alexa cried out and collapsed on the pavement. Her mind threatened to split in two.

The monster was going to rip her apart.

She was carried back to the car and placed, writhing and weeping, in the backseat. Unable to resist the waves of agony racking her body, Alexa lost all sense of time and space. Doors slammed. The monster roared through her skull. She sensed the car picking up speed. The road rumbled beneath her. A blurred world spun past the windows.

The monster twisted beneath her skull, making a nest of her gray matter, and whispered into her ears, YOU CANNOT RUN. WE WILL FIND YOU. YOUR END IS NEAR.

Una's voice entered her mind. *You are all we have between life and total annihilation, Alexa Baxter. Fight with everything you have.*

Alexa whimpered in response. She grasped to consciousness with everything she had left and prayed to anyone, anything that might listen to her.

Chapter Twenty-Eight

ALEXA WATCHED THE LANDSCAPE roll by as she held tight to the waking world. The monster continued to rip her from the inside out. She gleamed hot and electric, covered in sweat and standing on the knife's edge of possession.

Hot yet freezing, Alexa used the fresh sweatshirt to mop sweat from her face and held it tight when the pain grew too great. The shirt held a whiff of Sid's scent. She pressed that part to her nose to find comfort amidst the agonizing storm.

Mateo played a steady flow of Alexa's favorite bands over the car speakers. Billy Corgan crooned and wailed. Alice in Chains groaned about heroin's toll on their bandmates. Beck explained he was a loser and didn't have the right to live. Alexa murmured along, her voice strong on a few favored refrains and softer between unsteady bridges.

Una didn't bother hiding anymore. Emboldened by the monster's assault and the nearness of their destination, the unicorn refused to listen to anyone. Una grumbled when they didn't move fast enough and poked Alexa every time she closed her eyes for longer than five seconds.

Mateo had removed the headrest between himself and Alexa to monitor her better. Every so often, he reached back, tugged the hem of her soaked t-shirt, and whispered affirmations about her strength and resilience.

Sid's eyes shifted between rage and resignation as they continued the journey he had been ready to cancel hours before. The encounter with the monster had left him deeply unsettled. All plans had been called off the moment he woke panting in a cemetery, having no idea how he or anyone else got there in the first place. Calling their parents had been no more than a useless exercise.

As the shadows of early afternoon elongated, Alexa uttered a tangled cacophony of phrases making sense to no one but her. The monster whispered a continuous thread of threats and curses as Alexa maintained her resistance. Each time the monster reared within her, she sang loudly and off-key to her music. The monster's fury eventually settled into a low growl of angry diatribes.

Una had perched itself next to her lap, listening with quiet fascination to Alexa's battle. The unicorn added its own bits of encouragement when the monster quieted as they crossed the border from Nevada to Oregon.

"If I had a pencil, I would have to sharpen it every other stroke to draw all that brittle grass." Alexa traced the mountains in the distance against the window glass. She pictured using her smudge stick to soften shadows. A 6B or 8B pencil would be ideal for the darkest areas.

"Oh, hey," Mateo said. "You made sense right there. Good for you."

Looping gray strands of cloud danced across the sky. Alexa slapped at them, asking the monster to make them go away. Her veins popped in her hands like blue rivers against her pale flesh.

"Am I turning colors?" she asked Mateo.

His eyes grew wide before he caught himself. "No, Lex, you're the same girl you've always been. My sister from another mister."

Alexa hummed to "Blister in the Sun" as the sky swelled. Later, when "Creep" played, she laughed to herself. It was such an appropriate song for their journey. She floated along the melody line and joined Thom York's aching, raspy vocals.

She bobbed her head along with the chorus. "Do you see it, Mateo? The sky is gray like the song."

"Please tell me we're getting close." Mateo dropped his head against the top of the seat.

"Hey, Una, we there yet?" Alexa turned toward the unicorn's shining body. The unicorn shone as bright as the sun. "Ugh, turn the light off."

I know this is difficult for you, Alexa Baxter. I can see how the monster's influence affects your mental and physical capacity. I admire you. I had no idea you could be so strong. We are indeed getting close. I swear I can almost smell the Rift.

"Una can smell it." Alexa giggled. Another fleeting touch of clarity brought her hands to her bruised throat. She sucked in a sharp intake of breath. "God, I hope so. I don't know how much longer I can stay here."

"Stay here?" Sid barked from the driver's seat. He had been monosyllabic since the incident with the monster.

"I could disappear any second." Alexa sat back and closed her eyes. Una immediately pressed the sharp tip of its horn into her shoulder. "Ow, Una. I'm trying. Dammit."

They will try to convince you that they are right. I imagine they have already told you that I am the monster, not them. Do not trust them. Fight, Alexa Baxter. Fight their darkness.

Alexa shaded her eyes against the unicorn's dazzle. She tossed back another cold mouthful of water. "Tell me a story."

My stories are all too sad.

"That's okay. I like all sorts of stories. Can you tell me about your family? Or maybe a memory from when you were an itty-bitty unicorn."

You should focus on staying awake.

"Please. I need a distraction. Please."

The road whooshed beneath them. Above, the hole in the ceiling wailed a thin, aching strain. She tried sticking her pinky into the hole, but her hands shook too much. She dropped her hands, pulled her knees to her chest, and scratched at her forehead.

"Owie." Alexa pulled her hand away, frowning at the blood staining her fingertips.

Very well, Alexa. I see how hard you struggle. The Bright One's home world is long gone, but we like to tell stories of the time we did. A time so far in the past, it lives outside of time. A history grown legend. We call our lost world The Bright Place. And we continue to seek a new one even as we fight our annihilation.

We have little literature and little recorded history, so we pass on everything we know through our stories. And I can tell you very little. We do not believe others have the right to know us, to know our recognized truths.

Alexa envisioned great hordes of unicorns racing across the Milky Way, crying for their lost home—a dazzling array, winking and dancing like fallen stars.

"And you can't fight back?" Alexa said.

We tried. We failed. There is no more fighting back. Only escape or death.

"Well, that's a major bummer," Alexa said. What would it be like to live that sort of life? Forever driving her car into the hills, the mountains, even into the ocean. Leaping between the veils of reality. Falling into bizarre, unknowable places. Stuck in a bathroom at an uncomfortable angle.

Alexa giggled again, stuffed a fist against her mouth, and muttered, "Just until tonight. Hang on, Lex. Hang on."

Chapter Twenty-Nine

HOURS PASSED. TRAFFIC remained sparse. The world rolled past them on repeat: sand and scrub, then more sand and scrub. As the sun paced the sky, a line of green emerged in the distance—a promise of something new.

Una could not contain its excitement. Ears twitching, nostrils flaring, the unicorn stared out the window, its horn etching shapes into the glass pane. Una's tail had a mind of its own, occasionally knocking Alexa in the face.

Mateo and Sid were messaging each other on their phones with increasing frequency. They exchanged glances, nods, and mouthed words. Alexa didn't have it in her to care. Lost in creeping shadows, she had bigger things to worry about, and Una was too distracted to notice.

Alexa's fever ebbed and flowed. Her joints ached from the monster's roadside attack. Whispers played in her ears and leaped through her thoughts. Her weary mind traveled back to when she was a little girl playing with toys, acting out fantasy and adventure stories. Somehow, her little unicorn figurine had ended up in the car's back seat with her. What was the name she gave the toy so long ago? Stardust? Starlight? Starshine?

"Stardancer," she whispered.

When did she stop playing with Stardancer? When did books, music, and art overtake her interests? She couldn't pinpoint the change, like she couldn't pinpoint when the monster went from an itch in her forehead to a full-blown creature kneading her brain. She stood balanced on a precipice, her feet half-on and half-off the edge. Why didn't the monster simply overtake her like they had with the others?

SOMETHING FASCINATING.

A voice not belonging to Una turned over and over in an endless phrase within her skull. What was fascinating?

"Something fascinating," Alexa drawled. "Oh, now I see. I see." She smiled behind her bandaged hands because she knew something the monster knew: they would do horrible things to all of them at the end of their journey.

The monster quivered in her skull. WE ARE NEAR, WAITING FOR YOUR LOCATION. RUN AS FAST AS YOU WANT, BUT WE ARE A PART OF YOU NOW. YOU CANNOT RUN FROM WHAT IS INSIDE YOU.

"I don't want this," Alexa croaked, speaking to the monster. She sensed the monster growing past her head, oozing into her veins.

YOU TOOK THIS UPON YOURSELF WHEN YOU AIDED THE BRIGHT ONE. YOU SHOULD HAVE NEVER RUN. YOU DO NOT UNDERSTAND THE FOUL CREATURE YOU ARE HELPING.

"How could we know?" She hissed back with unexpected force. The monster may overtake her, but she would keep fighting until the bitter end.

"Lex?" Mateo said.

Una nudged her knee with its snout. *Who are you speaking to, Alexa? Is it the monster?*

"No biggie, just the monster in my head," Alexa giggled and let out a long sigh.

"Cool." Mateo pursed his lips and glared at Una. "How much closer, Bright One?"

We will arrive near sunset.

"Oh, that's good." Alexa ran a hand through Una's flaxen mane. "Una said near sunset, so that's great. I can't deal with this much longer."

"Well, that's great news," Mateo said.

Una sniffed Alexa, its whiskers tickling Alexa's face. *You must fight harder. They are sinking deeper into your body. I smell the monster all over you.*

Alexa shrugged. "I'm just a lowly Earth creature. I'm doing the best I can."

We are so close, Una repeated for the umpteenth time that day. The unicorn twisted away, its horn nearly gouging Alexa and Sid as it scrambled for a better view out its window.

Alexa's eyelids were heavy. Small weights hung from each lid. Una was so distracted by their progress, the Bright One didn't notice when Alexa let go. She sunk into her seat and tumbled back into the misty void where she had last spoken to the monster.

This time, Alexa would try a different tactic. The monster was winning, and she couldn't fight much longer. The two of them needed to talk, to parley, to try to find some sort of common ground or compromise.

In a voice for the monster's ears, she said, "I know we're close, but I think we won't know the final destination until we've arrived. Una can't tell us. It doesn't know our world. If you promise not to hurt my friends, I'll tell you where we are when I know."

WE MAKE NO PROMISES. YOU HAVE ASSISTED ONE OF THE MOST DANGEROUS FUGETIVES IN THE MULTIVERSE. THERE CAN BE NO COMPROMISE. YOU ALL SHOULD BE PUNISHED.

"We didn't know any better. How could you expect us to know better? Until a few days ago, I knew nothing about Bright Ones, monsters, or multiverses. It's not fair."

IGNORANCE DOES NOT PREVENT YOU FROM BEING COMPLICIT. YOU SHOULD HAVE ALLOWED US TO TAKE THE BRIGHT ONE WHEN WE FIRST ARRIVED. TO RUN IS TO ACCEPT GUILT. ALL THOSE WHO HELP THE BRIGHT ONES DESERVE THE SAME FATE AT THEM.

"Can't you see that Una is practically holding us hostage? I honestly don't know which one of you is worse. We have no choice but to keep going. We can't tell you where we are going because we don't fucking know. Be reasonable,"

WE DO NOT NEGOTIATE WITH THOSE WHO ASSIST FUGITIVES.

"You are a part of me, and you can see I'm telling the truth. You think I can lie when you're in my body? You know what I am, who I am. Give us a chance."

The monster fell silent, sliding around inside her ethereal form. The quiet stretched as the monster appeared to contemplate her words.

A crack of hot-green light struck her sightless eyes. The monster poured itself into every part of her, knocking away the remaining walls of resistance. The monster's talons were everywhere. At her throat, her stomach, her arms, writhing across her head.

"Stop, please. Not like this!" Alexa screamed.

Real hands shook her shoulders and called her name. She forced her eyes open, but the monster clouded her vision.

Mateo's voice whispered in her ear, "Lex. You have to pull out of it. Fight. Fight for all of us."

Clawing through the thin, elastic membrane between the void and the real world, she pushed the monster from her vision. "Stop it. You can't do this."

The monster let out a faint roar, and, like the sun burning away the morning fog, they curled back into the tiny space beneath her forehead.

Alexa inhaled a great breath, able to see the world with her own eyes again. She quickly realized the Civic was pulled over on the side of the interstate. A semi roared past. Mateo hovered over her. Sid was also there, looking over Mateo's shoulder.

Una was curled at her side, sniffing her head. *The monster seems to have receded.*

"Well, that was freaking wild." Alexa ran her fingers through her sweat-soaked hair.

"You scared the shit out of us, Lex." Mateo warily eyeballed Una. Alexa noticed the unicorn's horn pointing at his heart. "You started, like, having a seizure or something, so we pulled over. I think we should take you to the nearest hospital. I thought you were dying."

Excellent work, Alexa. Once again, you have proved to be the great exception to all I have heard about Earth. Now, we must keep going. You can seek medical attention once I am gone. Una's defiant gaze cut into Mateo and Sid.

"Honestly, I feel a lot better." Alexa waved everyone away from her. "Can you all give me a little room?"

Very well, Alexa Baxter. Una snorted and shifted off her lap. *You are fine. We must keep going.*

"Lex, there's a hospital over an hour from here. We should head that way." Sid crossed his arms over his chest, staring at the unicorn in barely bridled fury.

Do not listen to that silly boy. I cannot stop when I am so close to finally leaving this terrible world.

"I have a proposal." Alexa mopped her face with the sleeve of her sweatshirt. "If we don't get to the Rift by the end of the day, then we find the nearest hospital. How does that sound?"

I accept. We have mere hours left. Now, can we continue?

"Is this alien worth your life?" Sid smacked the door frame.

"Are you sure?" Mateo said. "I mean, I seriously thought you might be dying, Lex. I can't lose you. This isn't worth it."

Coward. I will drive my horn—

"Una, that's enough." Alexa held up a hand. The monster had pulled back for a reason. The time had come to let whatever was about to happen, happen. "We'll be there in a few hours. Let's get this over with."

"Okay." Mateo nodded and wiped the tears from his face. "A few hours isn't that much."

"I don't like this." Sid shook his head, a dark expression on his face.

"I know." Alexa sat up and smoothed her shirt. "I don't either. We're close, Sid. Please, do this for me?"

"Whatever," Sid murmured, carefully shutting Alexa's door before heading back to the driver's side.

Mateo and Sid took their seats and shut their doors in unison. Sid started the car, his lovely face twisted in anger. Like so many times before, after dealing with another heart-stopping incident, everyone in the car fell silent as they merged back into traffic.

Chapter Thirty

THE WORLD CHANGED AGAIN, becoming mountainous stretches of forest. Soft, sweeping puffs dotted the pinking sky. The change in scenery was a wonderful distraction for the three teenagers. The wind whistling through the ceiling hole perforated the silence.

The road signs informed Alexa that they had passed through Fremont National Forest and then Winema National Forest. Green still clung in dense patches throughout the land, though winter sprinkled distant mountain peaks.

Una's agitation grew nearly intolerable. The unicorn's tail slapped a steady rhythm against the passenger door. Una's coat shivered as if invisible flies landed on its flawless pelt. Alexa attempted once or twice to soothe the anxious beast, but Una snapped its teeth in response.

I am sorry, Alexa. I cannot help it. I may get off this terrible world alive.

Mateo switched the music from Alexa's maudlin grunge to hopeful pop tracks. After so many days on the road, Sid admitted that he was getting sick of both.

"So, what's your poison?" Mateo asked.

Sid said with a shy smile, "I love old-school hip-hop."

Grinning wickedly, Mateo played, "Ice, Ice, Baby."

In the way only music could, the song sent them down the road with a new lightness in their hearts. Soon, they ripped through a series of rap classics from Biggie Smalls, Tupac, and Jay-Z. Even Alexa, who claimed not to "get" rap music, giggled in appreciation as Sid knew the lyrics to almost every song they played.

Una trembled in the backseat as it fed Alexa directions. The unicorn had long ago cared about hiding itself. At one point, they passed a girl, roughly twelve years old, who nearly fell off her bike when she caught Una snorting out the window at an intersection.

Finally, a small but important sign popped into view. Alexa could feel it in her bones when she recognized their final destination. She had stumbled upon the location in the past when some listicle named off the United States' strange and magical natural phenomena. They passed a sign indicating the south entrance was open. She hoped the park kept late hours. What if they had come all this way and couldn't get in?

They passed another small town with a handful of motels and then headed north. They crossed meandering streams and small herds of cows grazing the countryside. Snow-topped mountains soared against the magenta twilight, and the world grew so beautiful Alexa's heart ached to draw it all.

They turned down the music and opened their windows. Cool mountain air glanced at their cheeks. The road shifted and they reached the entrance.

"Crater Lake National Park?" Mateo turned back to Una and Alexa. The name didn't appear to mean anything to him or Sid as he slowed down to enter the park.

"Yeah." Alexa leaned forward. "This is it."

Ponderosa pines towered above them as the sky faded closer to sunset. The Rift had to be located somewhere near the lake. Una stuck its head out its window, nostrils flared. They passed dirty banks of half-melted snow and continued deeper into the park.

The nearer they drew to the lake, the slower the speed limit and the more on edge both Alexa and Una grew. The unicorn bounced and nickered beside her. Alexa couldn't put into words her agitation; the unicorn wasn't the source of her unrest. Anxiety cramped her guts and tingled down her fingers. Something wonderful and awful lay around the bend.

The tree parted and revealed the extraordinary lake at the top of a mountain range.

"Oh, whoa," Mateo gasped.

Everyone turned to appreciate the dazzling sunset over Crater Lake. The water had turned the color of the molten gold sky. Pink-tinged clouds floated across the lake's mirrored surface as if great leviathans floated across its endless depths.

"We made it," Alexa whispered, clutching her hands in relief.

They reached a lookout point, and Una nearly jumped out the window. The rumble in its throat grew into a desperate growl.

"I guess we'll stop here." Sid found the nearest parking spot. They were the only vehicles in sight.

I need to get out. Immediately. Open the door.

Sid parked the car and opened Una's door before the Bright One accidentally impaled someone. The view was like taking a glimpse of heaven. As Una paced around the small parking lot, the three humans stood shoulder to shoulder and admired the glory of nature.

Mateo wrapped an arm around Alexa and whispered, "Did you send the texts, Sid?"

"As soon as I saw the first sign." He checked his phone. "I think at least one of them got through. There's no service up here. We won't know until we know."

"Did you get an odd feeling when you saw the sign too?" Alexa said as Una sniffed the air and flicked its ears in every possible direction.

Sid said, "When I saw the second sign telling us Crater Lake was thirty miles away, yeah."

They collectively monitored the Bright One's inspection as it paced the edges of the parking lot.

"We should go now while it's distracted." Mateo jerked his chin toward the car.

Slowly, silently, they peeled away from each other, taking soft, measured steps toward the Civic. Alexa glanced over her shoulder the whole time, but Una appeared preoccupied. All three of them winced when the automatic locks clicked open. Una let out a wailing cry and galloped after them.

We have to go to the island, Una shrieked, tossing its head. The unicorn lowered its horn in Alexa's direction. *I need you to come with me.*

"You don't need our help anymore." Alexa's stomach clenched. She clutched the passenger-side door handle. So close. Freedom lay so close at hand if the unicorn would let them leave.

"What did it say?" Mateo shouted from beside the trunk.

"Una wants me to go with it," Alexa said, her voice hitching as she spoke. "The Rift is on the island in the lake."

"Absolutely not," Sid barked from the other side of the car. He slapped the hood. "We did as you asked, now get the fuck outta here. The rest is your deal, not ours."

I insist you come with me. Una stepped closer to Alexa, horn-first.

"Please, Una, let me go home?" Alexa pleaded, noticing the tremble in the unicorn's legs. Was Una angry, or was the trembling something else?

The thought of scrambling alongside the edge of the mountaintop turned Alexa's stomach. She was a living ruin from her various attacks. Her eyes followed the trail they would take to reach the lakeshore nearest the island. The distance made her stomach turn.

Do not make me do this alone, Alexa Baxter. Walk with me to the lake. Please.

Was Una scared? "Una, you don't need me. You're strong. You can do this on your own."

"Lex, don't you dare go down that hill. It's suicide." Mateo quivered like Una.

Alexa sucked down a breath. Could she handle one last undertaking?

"I might be able to make it," Alexa suggested as bile rose in her throat. She let go of the door handle and tucked her cold hands in her pockets. She shivered beneath her sweatshirt, still damp from hours of sweating in the back seat. None of them were dressed to hike at night in the mountains.

"No way." Mateo stepped over to Alexa and wrapped his arms around her. "She's not going anywhere. Do it by yourself."

Una snorted and lowered its head. The unicorn pawed the earth and squared its shoulder like a bull preparing to charge. Nothing stood between Alexa, Mateo, and the unicorn.

Alexa Baxter, I demand you go with me. It is the last thing I need you to do, and then you will never see me again.

"But why? Why do I have to go with you?"

I will harm your dear Mateo if you do not.

"We can't trust it. We should have never trusted it." Mateo wrapped his arms tighter around Alexa.

"I know." Alexa shook and hugged Mateo tight. "Una will hurt you if I don't."

Chapter Thirty-One

ALEXA BAXTER, IF YOU *don't come with me, I will kill them both.* Una turned its shining eyes upon Alexa, and she swore the unicorn was pleading when it said, *Please, do not want to go alone.*

"Una, is that why?" Alexa was startled by the unicorn's vulnerability. "Why can't you just say that? You don't have to threaten me to get what you want."

Between Una's threats and her friends' refusal to follow the unicorn's orders, Alexa almost forgot the monster still living in her head. What she had mistaken for retreat turned out to be something completely different. The monster wasn't licking hidden wounds, for those wounds had never existed.

A spasm jolted through her body, and her brain cleaved in two. She dropped to the ground as the monster gripped her brain so tight, she was sure her head was about to explode. The boys' shouts and the unicorn's threats were insignificant compared to the monster sliding her conscience aside and taking control of her body.

STAY CALM, said the monster. THIS WILL ALL BE OVER SOON.

Alexa and the monster shared one mind and one body. Their wants and intentions rang out in awful clarity. The monster had waited for the right moment to take Alexa. As their two minds converged, Alexa's suspicions were proven correct: Una, the Bright One, was an extraordinarily dangerous beast, and it was a miracle that the teenagers were all still alive. The monster wasn't simply out to destroy Una but to protect the multiverse from the Bright One. The monster could indeed divide itself into multiple parts, and the rest of the collective wasn't far but required more time to reach them.

I AM SORRY TO DO THIS. I HOPE YOU WILL UNDERSTAND. With one final heave, the monster pushed Alexa into the corner of her brain. Alexa saw everything happen with her own eyes but had no control over her body or her voice. She was simply a passenger on the ride.

Mateo stood over her when her vision cleared. "Are you okay?" The worry in his eyes turned to horror as he saw the monster within. "Holy shit. Not you, too."

Alexa sensed cascading power running through her possessed body. The cold air became insignificant, and the limitations of her bruised body diminished. She sat up and leaped to her feet. A voice that was not her own said, "THIS MIGHT WORK."

The monster tested her body, flexing arms that didn't ache and stretched her previously stiff back. Alexa had never felt more invincible.

I feared this may happen. Una lashed its tail, eyes blazing. *I wish you had not done that to my Alexa Baxter. She does not deserve to be your vessel.*

"SURRENDER BRIGHT ONE," Alexa bellowed in a voice too big for her little body. "ALL THIS CAN END RIGHT HERE."

You will never take me alive. The unicorn attacked. With unnatural speed, Alexa easily dodged the charging Bright One and threw a shoulder into Una's side as it raced past her. Una lost its footing, stumbled, and fell into the surrounding decorative fencing.

Mateo reached toward Alexa. "Please! No, leave her alone!"

"You can fight the monster, just like me," Sid shouted as he ran around the Civic's trunk.

"CALM YOURSELF YOUNG EARTH CREATURES," The monster said. "SHE IS THE PERFECT TOOL FOR WHAT WE NEED TO DO. THIS WILL ALL BE OVER SOON."

Indeed monster. The time has come for this to end. Through Alexa's possessed body, the monster sensed Una's build-up of strength.

The sun had set, and daylight was no more than a faint glow on the horizon. The monster's power intensified her vision, and everything could be seen with perfect clarity. Sid and Mateo screamed for her. Alexa wished she could pull out of her corner and call back.

You may be powerful, but I am much faster than you in that mortal shape. Una lashed its tail.

Instead of wheeling around and going in for another attack, Una bolted toward the split-rail fence surrounding the parking lot and leaped into the rocky beyond. The monster and Alexa surged forward, muscles pumping with a fresh infusion of unworldly strength, and followed the unicorn into the darkness.

Chapter Thirty-Two

THE MONSTER TOOK ALEXA'S body and hurled her feet-first into the snow-patched ravine surrounding the lake. Alexa, deep within, screamed in complete and utter terror. The monster's possession was still new. They tumbled rather than chased the unicorn down the ravine.

SUCH AN UNWIELDY SHAPE, the monster complained when they regained footing. APOLOGIES, ALEXA BAXTER. WE SHALL TRY TO BE MORE CAREFUL.

Alexa gasped as she, being one with the monster, realized they didn't plan to hurt her or her friends after all.

YES, WE MEAN YOU NO HARM, the monster spoke in her mind, grunting as they leaped across a rocky outcropping. WE STUDIED YOUR INNER CONSCIOUSNESS. YOU ARE GOOD, ALEXA BAXTER. AND WE SEE HOW THE BRIGHT ONE TRICKED YOU.

Una shone through the woods despite the dark, moving with unspeakable grace across the uneven incline. Meanwhile, Alexa, who was not just Alexa, fought to stay upright as they pursued the unicorn. She scraped her knees and tumbled through snowbanks, but such distractions did not concern the monster. There was only the monster, the target, and the desired outcome.

Alexa's friends shouted behind her, their cries distorted by the surrounding landscape. She and the monster paused for a moment, staring back at the silhouettes of the screaming boys. Another movement caught their eye. Did Alexa hear sirens in the distance? Sid and Mateo's texts must have gone through, after all.

The monster cared little about other Earth creatures and continued their chase. Alexa fought between conflicted feelings as they pursued Una. What was the whole point of their journey if Una ended up destroyed by the monster in the end? Everything they had done had been in vain.

I SHALL EXPLAIN. Racing across an uneven incline of boulders, the monster told Alexa their version of the Bright Ones. The monster wasn't really a monster but a hired assassin—a multiverse-renowned mercenary.

The Bright Ones cut a different picture in the monster's version of the multiverse. The Bright Ones weren't just nomads but were invaders. Destroyers. A cancer spreading from one world to the next as they attempted to claim a new home. And with each home they claimed, the Bright Ones burned through each planet's resources.

Alexa gasped as the monster fed her images of lush, green worlds reduced to withered, moldering ash. So that's what happened to Alexa's backyard and flowers in the cemetery. The Bright Ones' most efficient way of feeding themselves was drawing out the life forces of living things. They left nothing but death in their wake.

AND NOW YOU SEE, FOR THE SAKE OF ALL, WE CANNOT ALLOW THEM TO LIVE, the monster said. Alexa understood what the monster showed her, and yet she understood Una too. The unicorn had done whatever it took to live. Wouldn't Alexa do the same?

According to the monster, if Alexa had walked down Crater Lake's embankment under her own power like Una wanted her to do, the unicorn would have killed her once they reached the island. Or did Una just want a friend to walk with a little further before leaving Alexa behind forever?

They reached the edge of the lake. The island was a forested shadow in the near distance. The lake was a giant mirror, reflecting everything from the mountains to the darkening heavens. Una trotted into the water to its knees and wailed at the intense cold. Una's cry reached into Alexa's heart. Alexa didn't care what the unicorn had done in the past. She didn't want to monster to hurt the Bright One.

Possessed by the monster, Alexa could now sense the Rift too. The portal plucked at her limbs, calling out to her from across the water. The multiverse was connected through a massive system of Rifts. Hundreds of them, no, millions. The intergalactic, interdimensional super highway.

Alexa Baxter, do not stop fighting. You can still save me! The unicorn bolted out of the frigid water and shook out its coat. *Do not believe the monster's lies. They cannot be trusted. The monster will take me first and then take you.*

"YOU HAVE FOOLED THEM LONG ENOUGH, BRIGHT ONE. I CANNOT LIE TO YOU, ALEXA BAXTER, NOT WHEN WE SHARE THE SAME MIND."

In her heart, Alexa knew the monster spoke the truth, or at least what they believed to be the truth. If she had learned anything during their adventure out west, it was that many truths existed simultaneously, even those contradicting each other.

Very well. I am sorry, Alexa Baxter. I never meant to hurt you. Una lowered its horn, preparing to charge. *You showed me nothing but kindness. Even when I was cruel. I will never forget you.*

Alexa silently cried out, begging for the unicorn to give up and save itself, but the monster had rendered her mute.

"AS YOU CAN SEE, YOU CANNOT REACH THE RIFT." The monster gestured to the island. "THE WATER IS TOO COLD. EVEN FOR YOU."

I refuse to submit. Una bucked in place.

"COME QUIETLY AND THEY MAY LET YOU LIVE. RESIST AND DIE."

In a cage? For the rest of my life? Tortured for information? You cannot be serious. Una paced along the narrow, rocky shore.

"THIS IS MY LAST OFFER, BRIGHT ONE."

Una charged, raising a myriad of unintelligible curses. Alexa silently cried out, fearing for everyone's life. A bolt of green lightning cut across the sky. The monster roared in triumph as the rest of their collective fell from the heavens in a roiling, thundering cloud of darkness.

At the same instant, the monster released Alexa, tossing her aside like a sack of flour onto the cold, wet ground. The loss of the monster's strength left Alexa as she had always been: a weak little human. The fall knocked the wind out of her, leaving her withing on her side, gasping for air while a science fiction movie raged before her.

The monster descended from the heavens like a great hand, reaching to snatch Una from the earth. Una screamed, plunging desperately back into the cold lake.

"Una!" Alexa cried out, reaching for the unicorn.

The unicorn, who wasn't a unicorn, reared up to accept the monster's fingers crashing around it, obliterating Una from her sight. Surges of green lightning threaded the roiling mist, briefly illuminating the shape of the unicorn at its core. The light gathered at the monster's center and exploded. A cry of agony burst from the center of the cloud monster. Alexa pressed her hands to her ears and joined Una's wail with her own.

The monster obliterated Una like they had many other Bright Ones. While the monster was in Alexa's head, they had shown her how they would destroy Una. Similar to her dreams, the monster poured itself into every orifice, filling the Bright One until its bones and tissue could no longer hold. In the end, nothing was left of Una but red mist.

Time slowed, impossible to measure. Una's death cry faded into the night. The battle that had lasted minutes could have been over a hundred years as Alexa held her aching head and wept into the freezing sand beneath her.

The cold was intolerable. Lake water, snow, and mud soaked Alexa, and every part of her throbbed.

"Alexa?" A voice shouted from above. "Can you hear me?"

Another voice joined. "Alexa Baxter, where are you?"

More shouts echoed from the top of the hill. Alexa looked up to see dozens of flashing lights and silhouettes of people waving in her direction. She tried to sit up but didn't have the strength. The once glorious sensation of the monster's power had left her a broken husk.

At first, it appeared the monster had left their world and gone elsewhere. But, though barely visible, the monster stood several feet away from her, hovering above Crater Lake, a spot of pure darkness in the already dark world.

No, not really a monster. They were called a Brume. A race of creatures whose specialty was to seek and destroy each target given for a hefty fee. Alexa clutched her chest. Did Una deserve to die? The monster claimed there was no other choice and had shown her as much. Una's final scream continued to ring in her ears.

WE ARE SORRY YOU HAD TO GO THROUGH THIS. The churning mass of darkness hovered closer. THE BRIGHT ONE GAVE US NO OTHER CHOICE.

Alexa was so cold, so tired. She wanted to take a nap until her friends came down to help.

WHEN YOU OPEN YOUR EYES AGAIN, ALL OF THIS WILL BE GONE.

More shouts and sirens. The sound of feet shuffling down the rocky incline. They would never find her in time. As cold turned to warmth, everything faded. She couldn't hang on.

"What ... what do you mean?"

The monster drew nearer. ALL THIS WILL BE NOTHING MORE THAN A DREAM WHEN YOU WAKE. LESS THAN A DREAM. JUST LIKE THE WAITRESS AND THE OFFICER, WHAT YOU WENT THROUGH THE LAST FEW DAYS WILL BE NO MORE BUT LOST TIME. YOU WILL HAVE

FORGOTTEN EVERYTHING AND NEVER HEAR FROM US AGAIN.

"I ... what? I don't—"

Everything grew faint. Reality lost structure. No more unicorns, monsters, or intergalactic drama. Just Alexa, one, next to a lake atop a mountain.

REST NOW, ALEXA BAXTER. AND FORGET US.

Chapter Thirty-Three

LIGHT PLUCKED ALEXA'S eyes. The desire to bury her head under the blankets and go back to sleep permeated every part of her.

A persistent beeping pulsed nearby. Alexa frowned. Where did that come from? She reached to clap her hands over her ears. "Ugh, can someone get the alarm?"

Her body protested every movement. Every joint ached. Why was she in so much pain?

"Alexa?" A kind voice punctuated the beeping soundscape.

A hand rested on hers. Even Alexa's hands ached, skin tight as she tried to flex her fingers. What the hell? She pressed her other hand to her forehead. The light itched at her eyelids.

Alexa knew what it was like to have an itch that refused to go away.

Why? What a strange thought. What else did she remember? Feeling cold for a very, very long time, but why? Winter was right around the corner, and she hated to go outdoors without a proper jacket.

"Alexa." the voice repeated.

"Hmm?" Alexa blinked and flinched. She grasped the hand holding hers.

"Alexa, honey, can you open your eyes?" Alexa's mother said.

"I think so." Alexa's tongue scraped along the inside of her mouth. Her stomach throbbed, aching for nourishment.

"Lex?"

Mateo's voice. Why was Mateo in her bedroom? Did he stay overnight? They usually slept in the basement during their slumber parties.

"What?" Alexa blinked and peered into the bright, hazy world. She made out the silhouettes of three people standing around her bed.

A figure drew close. A woman with a clear voice asked Alexa random questions about how she felt, what hurt, and other inane things that irritated her. She did her best to respond, but none of it made much sense.

"The nurse is trying to help you," Cynthia's tight, exhausted voice explained. "Please answer the nurse's questions."

"Nurse?" Alexa tried to sit up but met with resistance. Various cords and an IV dangled from her. "Oh, whoa. What happened?"

Her mother's face expressed several conflicting emotions, and Alexa's stomach tightened. Whatever had happened must have been bad.

Mateo squatted next to her. "Hey, Lex."

Alexa curled up on her side and met her friend's worried eyes. "Hey."

Mateo gave her a tight smile but said nothing. His eyes switched between her and the other two adults in the room. Something was really wrong, and Alexa got the feeling it was better not to ask too many questions.

"They keep saying no one remembers anything," Her mother patted a tissue to puffy, red-rimmed eyes. Cynthia rarely cried.

"Hey, I'm going to leave you with your Mom." Mateo squeezed her hand.

"Sure, okay." Alexa squeezed back, hesitant to let him go.

"Don't worry. I'll be back soon." Bubbly Mateo had disappeared. Alexa opened her mouth to ask him what happened, but the look on her mother's face told her to keep quiet. From how Cynthia reacted when he stood beside her, Mateo had something to do with her ending up at the hospital.

Her father arrived soon after, looking more haggard than she had ever seen him. He gave her a tight smile and kissed her forehead, something he hadn't done since she was little.

"My mouth is, ugh, dry?" Alexa croaked.

"Have an ice chip." Cynthia placed a sweating plastic cup in her daughter's bandaged hands. Alexa dug out several broken pieces of ice and dropped them on her sandpaper tongue. The cold prompted the faint impression of a memory: wet rocks biting into her skin and cold pure air as she lay next to a body of water.

"Mom, how did I get here?" Alexa crunched the ice between her teeth.

"You don't remember either?" Cynthia's frown deepened.

"Remember what?" The splintering cold in her mouth felt good. She wiggled her hands and feet, but nothing appeared to be broken. Her legs ached, especially her knees. She was weak, exhausted, and something else she couldn't put her finger on.

"You were nearly in the third stage of hypothermia when they found you." Cynthia dragged one of the chairs next to

Alexa's bed. "You were out there in just a sweatshirt. No coat. What were you thinking?"

"I don't know?" Alexa shrugged. She didn't like being cold, and her usual stocking cap appeared missing. She brushed her fingers over her forehead and discovered a rough texture.

"They told me your heart rate was so low." Cynthia sucked in a sharp breath.

"Am I going to be okay?" Alexa said. What had happened to her? Something big had happened and left only sensations behind. Cold. Water. Pain.

"The most invasive thing they had to do was give you warmed IV fluids," said Cynthia.

"Did, I, like, fall in the St. Croix River or something?"

Her dad bounced up from the chair in the corner and hissed. "What the hell is going on? She doesn't remember either?"

Alexa had never seen her parents in such a state. "Either?"

"Tuesday night," her mother said, "I got a text from Mateo that you, he, and Sidhit Dayani had to take a friend in trouble out west. I assumed maybe to Sioux Falls, but certainly not on the other side of the country. All three of you gave us barely any details until Thursday evening. Just a constant stream of bullshit."

Alexa sat back in bed, baffled. Nothing her mother said made sense. What person? The opposite side of the country. And what did Sid have to do with anything about this? They barely spoke at school. He had no idea about her intense crush on him.

"Sid? Where am I? I'm not in Riverview?"

Her father continued, "You left your cell phone behind, so everything's been filtered through Mateo and Sidhit. Even Sidhit mother, who is really … intense, couldn't get a straight answer from her son."

Alexa's mind spun, trying to fit the impossible pieces together. "Sid was with me and Mateo?"

"Yes, but why?" Her father's voice rose as his agitation increased.

"I literally have no idea." Alexa wanted to curl up and toss the stiff bedsheets over her head. What had she done? Or what was done to her?

"Someone must know something," her father barked.

"Rodger, babe, you're making her upset." Cynthia held out her hand to her husband. "Now, Thursday night, we got another call from Sidhit's parents. Something about being at Crater Lake. Honey, why did you go there?"

"Crater Lake?" Alexa couldn't make sense of anything they said. Her ears buzzed, and her head ached. What day was it?

"And now, allegedly, no one remembers anything." Rodger dropped Cynthia's hand and paced at the foot of the hospital bed.

"They found you next to the lake, half-frozen." Cynthia twisted the bedsheets between her fingers. "They had to use ropes and all sorts of equipment to get you out of there. Thank God Dr. Dayani called the local police as soon as she knew where you were."

"And where am I?" Alexa said. "What day is it?"

"You're at Asante Rogue Regional Medical Center in Oregon," Alexa's mother said. "You left Tuesday evening, and it's now Saturday morning."

"Oregon? Saturday?" Alexa couldn't begin to understand her parents' story. She recalled a lake in the mountains at twilight, the sky purple, and the lake a perfect mirror.

"I think I need to close my eyes," Alexa whispered and buried her head into the hospital pillow. Nothing made sense. A road trip? With Mateo, sure, but Sid? How was such a thing possible, and why didn't she remember anything?

Her father grumbled and continued pacing his frustrations through the hospital suite. Her mother pushed her hair from her eyes and kissed her temple. Alexa let go and once more slipped into the waiting comfort of slumber.

For some odd reason, she dreamed of unicorns.

Chapter Thirty-Four

NONE OF IT MADE A BIT of sense—not to anyone, and especially not to Alexa. Parents were furious, and their kids were frightened and confused.

According to Mateo's sleuthing, Sid had a shallow stomach cut and couldn't remember anything from the past few days. Alexa was by far the most injured of the three. The marks on her neck indicated someone had tried to strangle her. For several hours police believed that either Sid or Mateo had done it to Alexa until she pointed out that the finger marks on her neck were considerably bigger than either Sid or Mateo's hands.

More interviews with the local police followed. Mateo, Sid, and Alexa's stories didn't change. Everyone offered to take blood tests despite the objection of Sid's family lawyer, and Alexa refused to press charges. Eventually, authorities told both boys and their families to "get out and never come back."

Mateo stopped by one last time before he and his mother hopped on a plane back to the Twin Cities. He crowded next to her hospital bed and whispered, "This is just insane. I can't wait to go home. I honestly feel like I've been gone forever, even though I don't remember anything."

"I wish I knew where these bruises came from." Alexa's fingers fluttered around her neck. "Dude had huge-ass hands. And speaking of hands," she turned the cuts healing across her palms in Mateo's direction. "Who or what the fuck did this?"

Mateo said, "The last thing I remember is Tuesday at lunch. You said you had something to show me, and you were being super weird about it."

"And I remember nothing after I left school Monday. There's, like, this weird empty hole in my brain, and a bunch of memories are just waiting to fill it."

"We'll catch up again at home," Mateo said. His mom called for him from the hospital room door. "Maybe we'll remember something by then."

Alexa held him for one last question. "And I heard my car is sort of a mess? There's a big hole in the roof and one in the trunk? But they don't look like bullet holes, according to the cops. What would do that? And what about Sid? Why was Sid with us?"

Mateo shook his head. "I tried to talk to him, but his parents were always around. They've decided to blame us for everything since Sid can do no wrong. I think they've already left."

"He probably hates us." Alexa pouted. She hadn't caught a glimpse of him during her recovery.

"You could try to talk to him at school?" Mateo started back-pedaling when his mother, Pilar, told him she would leave him behind if he didn't go with her immediately. "But, I think he'll avoid us like the plague."

A heavy feeling settled in Alexa's chest. Mateo was right. The tiny spark of hope Alexa once held disappeared. Now she would never be his friend, or more.

Left behind, Alexa tried to sleep, tried to think of nothing, but sleep was also a perilous place. She dreamed of bulbous, dark smoke and booming voices. And a unicorn, always a unicorn the size of a Great Dane.

The doctor released Alexa from the hospital Monday afternoon, expecting a full recovery. The bruises had begun to fade, and her cuts and scrapes were well on their way to healing. Alexa's parents decided to leave her car behind and sold it to a used car salesman. As Alexa dug through her Civic one last time, she witnessed first-hand the punctures in the ceiling and trunk and all over the backs of the two front seats. And someone had been scratching at the windows with something sharp.

Alexa picked up an empty container of Easy Mac among the energy drink cans and empty bottles of water. The container appeared licked clean, which sent a tingle through her brain and a unicorn racing through her thoughts. The same one from her dreams.

"Una," Alexa whispered as she turned the container in her hands and tossed it in the garbage. Where did that word come from? Was it a name?

After removing the rest of the garbage, Alexa tossed her balled-up, stinky, and still-damp Nirvana t-shirt in her suitcase with the two mysterious black sweatshirts from South Dakota and Nevada.

Instead of flying out of Portland, her parents decided on a more expedient flight out of Medford. Alexa observed her parents in the cramped terminal from a seat near their gate. She pulled her knees to her chest and tried not to spy on her parents. They quietly discussed how to move forward with Alexa. Her mother's voice cracked as she asked Rodger if they had failed their daughter. As someone who preferred to hang in the background, Alexa hated being subjected to so much scrutiny.

Alexa studied her last text exchange between herself and Mateo as a distraction. The question, *R there bears in Riverview,* seemed to be the place where everything started going sideways. Apparently, she had found something in the women's bathroom at Birkmose Park. Usually, Alexa wasn't so cryptic with her texts.

The gap in her memories contracted, and she vividly remembered standing outside the women's bathroom, grasping the outer door handle. Something was making a racket inside the bathroom. Who or what did she find?

Una. She had found Una there. But who was Una?

She turned up her music, letting Nirvana roar through her ears, and forced all else to disappear from her thoughts until they returned to Riverview.

Chapter Thirty-Five

ALEXA HAD NEVER BEEN so happy to be back in Riverview or so happy to be at her house. Her sister, Andrea, caught Alexa by surprise when she met them at the front door.

"You're here," Andrea murmured into her hair. "We were so worried."

Alexa swallowed a sob and leaned into the fierce pressure of her sister's hug. "I'm okay."

Andrea pulled back and wiped away a few tears. "That's good. That's really good."

Andrea took Alexa's suitcase from her hands and guided her into the house. Her parents piled in behind her, wavering on their feet. Cynthia dropped her bags at the base of the staircase, walked straight to her wine fridge, and poured a taller-than-usual glass of chardonnay before slumping into one of the kitchen chairs. Her father followed suit, pouring a generous glass of scotch and sitting in the chair opposite his wife.

The clock on the kitchen microwave read midnight. Andrea asked if anyone wanted a snack and offered to make sandwiches. Cynthia gave her daughter a grateful smile and nodded. Alexa yawned and shuffled over to the central island as Andrea removed sandwich fixings from the fridge. Andrea pulled out a loaf of local bakery bread. Alexa opened the plastic wrapping and stuffed the heel of the sourdough loaf into her mouth.

A memory flashed: Alexa grabbing several containers from the fridge and piling them right where Andrea now piled sandwich ingredients.

"Hey, did I, by chance, finish off Mom's leftover mac-and-cheese before I disappeared?" Alexa whispered to her sister.

"Yeah," Andrea said. "You ate, like, half-a-pan of leftovers. Mom was kinda pissed." her eyes widened, and she leaned in close. "Is that why Sid came over? For a snack?"

Alexa's chest swelled at his name. "I have no idea." However, at the same instant, Alexa recalled Sid entering the kitchen, all color draining from his face. What had caused such a reaction?

"He was back at school today." Andrea laid out a row of sandwich bread.

"Yeah?" Alexa settled into one of the bar seats, pulse racing. Her crush on Sid had changed. She had admired him from a distance for years, but somehow there was a deeper connection for a reason she didn't understand.

"Of all the guys to take on a cross-country joy ride." Andrea waggled her eyebrows and squeezed a dollop of mustard on a slice of bread.

Alexa's heart continued to thrum. "Did he say anything?"

"No. He won't say anything about any of it." Alexa's sister glanced over at her parents, who were entirely absorbed in their smartphones. "And, like, some of the soccer guys were talking shit about you, and he totally flipped out. Told them to fuck off. You sure you don't remember anything?"

"Gosh, I wish I did." Alexa sighed and shoved a chunk of vegan cheese in her mouth. She clutched the counter, sensing answers on the tip of her tongue. "Hey, I think I'm going to bed. I am so wiped out."

Cynthia stood and held out her arms. "I need a hug first."

Alexa hurried across the kitchen to be enveloped in her mother's strong embrace. Her mom always smelled good, and her hugs were firm but gentle. She could have stayed there forever.

"Now, get some rest." Cynthia released Alexa and studied her daughter for a long moment. "Are you sure you still want to go to school tomorrow? Maybe take a day off?"

"I think I'll go stir crazy sitting around here," Alexa said. "And I know I've said this a ton of times, but I'm sorry I scared you." Alexa hated showing emotion in front of her family, but there was no holding back. "I don't know how to make everything okay again, but I want to try."

"Right now, you need to heal and return to your normal schedule." Cynthia rubbed her daughter's shoulders, eyes fixed on Alexa's bruised neck. "You know, maybe it's best you don't remember."

"Yeah, I heard PTSD totally sucks," Andrea said as she tossed lettuce on sandwiches.

"Hey." Her father rose from his chair and also pulled Alexa into a hug. "We'll get through this together, no matter what 'this' is. Your mother might be right. Maybe forgetting is best."

Alexa leaned into her father's hug. "Yeah, you're probably right."

"But if anything comes back to you," Rodger said, his intense eyes locking on Alexa's. "Tell us immediately. Someone needs to be punished."

Alexa ducked out of his arms. "I tell you if I remember anything. 'Night, everybody."

She grabbed her suitcase and trudged up the stairs to her bedroom. When she snapped on the bedroom light, her room didn't feel the same either. Her eyes traced the familiar furniture and decor and landed on her plastic unicorn sitting atop her dresser.

"Stardancer." Alexa crossed her room and plucked the unicorn from its perch. She pressed the tip of her finger against the sharp little horn. For a moment, she pictured a different sort of unicorn, no bigger than a Great Dane, pointing its spiraling horn toward her chest. She shivered, and the image dissolved.

"Una." Was that the name of the unicorn racing through her thoughts and dreams the last couple of days? As Mateo would say, "That's insane."

Alexa left her suitcase with her coat and shoes in the middle of the floor. She flopped into bed, her first time on a comfortable mattress in nearly a week. How did she know that? Too many thoughts whirled through her mind.

The idea of facing Sid tomorrow at school filled her with an alternating combination of hope and dread. Why did he defend her? Or did he tell them off because he was embarrassed to be associated with her? Maybe he remembered something she didn't. Was she brave enough to ask?

Probably not.

Alexa clutched the plastic unicorn to her chest as she fell into a deep, empty sleep.

Chapter Thirty-Six

SHE WOKE THE NEXT MORNING to sunlight streaming through her window right where she belonged—home sweet home. The retro bedside alarm clock Mateo got her for her sixteenth birthday told the time. She had forgotten to set the alarm on her phone. For a half-second, she panicked, wondering how her mother let her sleep in so late. In the next half-second, a familiar but prominent ache in her legs and throat reminded her of the past two days.

Yawning, she rolled onto her back and stared at her ceiling. Who woke in her bed that morning? Would it be a silent, slinking shadow girl hovering in the background? Or a new, alien version of herself whose skin could barely contain her and was starting to believe in unicorns.

Alexa brought her hands to her face and studied the strips of cuts across her palms. She poked at the largest wound in her left hand. That one might leave a scar. The doctors had asked her about them so many times back in Oregon. Her parents mentioned bandaged hands at dinner, but Alexa had no memory of the meal.

No. Wait.

Una had done this to her hands. It hadn't meant to harm her. Or maybe the surly unicorn didn't bother to warn her.

Una. It. Why "it"? Why not she, or he, or they?

The blank space in her head quivered, threatening to open and let everything out. A creeping sensation danced down her back. Maybe she should do what her parents suggested and try to forget. Move on. Get back on schedule.

She tugged off her jeans from last night and surveyed the bruises and scrapes covering her legs, especially at her knees. Her arms were the same, with scrapes on the heels of her hands and elbows, like she had braced herself for a fall or two. A purple handprint covered her upper right arm. The hand of a large man surrounded by a halo of spinning lights, ready to do what was necessary to get to the truth.

Alexa gasped. She could feel his hands on her throat, his fingernails digging into the back of her neck. She buckled against her bed, letting the terrible sensations wash over her before tumbling back into the recesses of her mind.

Panting, she got back up, grabbed her suitcase, and tossed it onto the bed. Perhaps more answers lay among the artifacts from her journey. Alexa opened the large front panel where she had shoved all her shirts from her forgotten journey. She sorted through her t-shirt, the sweatshirt with a wolf, and the one from Nevada. A sparkle of light between the black folds caught her eye. Several long strands of flaxen white hair lay in the middle of her Nirvana shirt.

As she grasped the strands between her fingers, light refracted and dazzled them along their lengths. The strands were like pieces of fractured sunlight. She knew what these were. They belonged to Una. Una, the unicorn, wasn't a unicorn but an alien creature called a Bright One.

The closed door within her mind splintered with a silent bang. The information came in a torrent. Even though her eyes were wide open, images flickered in the place of her bedroom. Una, the unicorn trapped in the women's bathroom. A monster—no, a Brume—pouring from the sky and chasing them out of Rapid City. Mateo screaming her name as a possessed patrolman tossed Alexa onto the hood of his car. Sid standing so close she could smell his sweet breath as he brushed a sweaty lock of hair from her brow. The wail of Una as the monster ripped it apart.

She grasped her head, holding together the mental split through her brain. She writhed on the floor of her bedroom, her head raging in a way that reminded her of the Brume ripping her apart from the inside out.

The Brume didn't know the mental crack the unicorn created had altered her beyond anything the multiverse understood. They had tried to empty her mind, but the patch didn't hold. All of them had underestimated her, the weak, primitive Earth creature.

The crack didn't necessarily close, but the information stopped flowing into her brain, leaving her with more information than she wanted—enough to make a young woman go mad. The monsters had no idea that when they possessed her, they had revealed pieces of information hidden within their collective brains, too.

"No ... no, I don't want this." Alexa pushed herself to her feet and collapsed onto the bed. Worlds upon worlds existed beyond her own and the folds of Earth's reality. "Please stop." Alexa pressed her pillow over her ears as the Brume's roar cut against her skull.

The Brume had done her and her friends a favor by wiping their memories. The typical protocol was to destroy those exposed to the Bright One for fear of contamination and the spread of perceived contamination. And if they had any idea what she remembered, they would come back and destroy her.

The flood of information sent Alexa stumbling to the bathroom across the hall. Her stomach lurched, but only bile poured from her throat. She hated it when her mother was right: everything had been better when she didn't remember.

She stopped dry-heaving and slumped onto the woven mat next to the sink. The frantic footsteps of her mother thudded up the stairs. The last thing Alexa needed was her mother's questions while the knowledge of the multiverse knocked around her brain.

"Alexa?" Her mother's face peered through the open bathroom door.

Alexa reached over and flushed the toilet. "Yeah, sorry. I didn't mean to scare you."

Her mother was dressed for work in a beautifully tailored power suit. "Maybe going to school today is not such a good idea? Do you want me to make a call? You don't need to go if you're not ready."

"No, no." Alexa got up from the floor and sat on the toilet seat. "I can't be here by myself today. I need to feel normal."

Cynthia hesitated and placed a hand against her daughter's forehead. "You're not running a temperature."

Alexa brushed her mother's hand away and stepped over to the sink, ignoring the black spots floating in her vision. She was on the edge of possibly vomiting again or maybe even passing out, but she didn't want her mother to see her fall apart. She would go mad, stuck at home all day. She needed a distraction from the wild information flashing through her cracked brain.

"I mean it. I want to go to school," Alexa said. She turned on the faucet and splashed a handful of cold water onto her face.

"You're sure?" Her mother asked.

"Yeah. Absolutely sure."

"Okay, your choice." With a resigned sigh, her mother headed back to the hallway. "We're leaving in an hour. And you might want to grab a scarf from your sister's closet or mine. Your throat looks a horror."

Chapter Thirty-Seven

WALKING INTO SCHOOL was like walking into a waking dream. Everything was familiar and yet somewhat altered. The last time Alexa headed out the main doors of Riverview High, she had Mateo in tow, taking him to meet the impossible thing in her parent's backyard. Alexa stuck in her earbuds, turned up her favorite Radiohead song, and entered the lion's den.

Striding along the groove of "Creep," she sensed a hundred eyes on her. She had returned to school at lunchtime, the busiest time of day. Walking down the cafeteria's perimeter, dozens of heads turned to follow her progress. No one dared approach her, but they were happy to stare.

Radiohead continued to thump in her ears as she headed to where she typically hid during lunchtime: the art room.

Alexa felt a flood of relief when she found Mateo already there, where she hoped he would be. Silhouettes against the big windows, he jumped to his feet as soon as Alexa entered the art room.

"I wasn't sure if you were coming today." Mateo jumped from his seat and threw his arms around her. "You weren't answering your phone."

"Sorry." Alexa adjusted the only black scarf her sister owned. Unfortunately, it was also quite sparkly. "It's been a crazy morning."

"Bestie, the school is exploding," Mateo said. "And you're the bomb."

"Oh, God." Alexa groaned.

"Hey, Alexa." The two art teachers simultaneously popped their heads through the open door of their shared office. From how they shifted their feet and exchanged looks, they knew they wanted to say something but didn't know what.

"Hey." Alexa waved and forced a smile.

"How are you, uh, feeling?" Ms. Ash asked.

"Never better." Alexa widened her false grin until her cheeks ached. She unzipped her backpack and pulled out her lunch. "Thanks for asking."

"Well, if you need anything, don't hesitate to ask," said Ms. Ash.

Ms. Green nodded in vigorous agreement. "Yes, absolutely anything."

"Thanks." Alexa bowed her head to hide her shining eyes. The last thing she wanted to do was start crying in front of her teachers.

"Okay, great. Well, have a nice lunch." Ms. Ash tugged Ms. Green, and they went back into the office.

"Woof, this is going to be a long afternoon." Alexa headed to her regular seat. "Do they all talk to you like that? The teachers, I mean?"

"Yep." Mateo settled beside her; his lunch spread out across the table. Homemade tamales, his favorite—his mother must have forgiven him.

Alexa pulled out her lunch: cheese, tomato, sprouts and mayo on what was left of the sourdough loaf. She counted down the seconds before Mateo exploded beside her.

Three. Two. One.

"Oh my God," he trilled. "You should hear what everyone is saying. I've never had more attention whores come up to me. The gossips are out, and they're hungry."

So, Mateo remembered nothing. She needed to maintain the same stance for the time being. Alexa touched her sister's scarf. The memory of the police officer wrapping his hands around her neck slammed through her thoughts. Alexa dropped her sandwich and grasped the art table until the images faded.

"Whoa, where did you go there?" Mateo tugged the fringed end of Andrea's scarf.

"Nowhere." Alexa picked up her sandwich and took a big bite. She hadn't eaten much in the last week, and this was her first proper meal outside of the crappy hospital food.

"Everyone is being surprisingly chill about us missing school," Mateo said, his lunch forgotten and going cold. "I just have a bunch of makeup work due by the end of the week. All the teachers are being super nice. Even Mr. Huftile. I get the feeling they all think we were abducted, and all our peers think we went on a wild, drugged-out, cross-country party."

"Party? Ha. I guess that's better than how our parents reacted." She chewed another satisfying bite of the sandwich. She dug into her lunchbox to see what else her mother had packed and discovered a giant chocolate chip cookie. The signs were clear, her mother was more worried than angry.

How could she sit there with her best friend, eating lunch like nothing was a big deal after everything they had gone through? The monster had ripped the Bright One apart from the inside out. And Una's scream. She would never forget that gut-wrenching wail. Was this how her life was going to be now? Assaulted by one horrible memory after another?

"Lex, you okay?"

"Yeah, sort of. Sometimes I get these little flashes of memory." Alexa took another bite. At least she maintained her appetite despite everything.

"Really? Like what?"

"Just flashes. Big blue sky. Storm clouds. A lake on the top of a mountain." Eventually, she would spill the beans, but not all at once. Mateo would never believe what they had gone through.

"Anything else?" Mateo noisily sipped his Diet Coke.

Alexa took another big bite of the sandwich to avoid answering. For Mateo, the past week was a strange, forgotten adventure. She was glad he didn't remember. The knowledge within her was terrible. Maybe she shouldn't tell Mateo anything if they weren't supposed to remember. What if the Brumes found out, or the organization that had hired them—the MGA—the Multiverse Governing Association?

"Lex?"

Alexa swallowed. "It's all just a lot of jumbled nonsense in my brain. Have you, um, seen Sid around at all?"

Mateo wore a knowing grin. "He sort of waved at me when I passed him once in the hallway. But that's it. We talked a tiny bit at the hospital back in Oregon. He was so confused. So upset. His parents were so hard on him, and he didn't know what to do to make it better. His parents think we're lying."

Only one of them was a liar. Her.

"That's unfair," Alexa said. Yesterday she was as lost as the boys. And today, she knew too much.

Mateo said, "Mom's taking this pretty well, considering. I think she's mad about me spending money more than anything else. I sat down last night and reviewed all my online bank receipts. We went from Minnesota to South Dakota, then Wyoming, possibly Utah and Nevada, and then we ended up at Crater Lake. Quite the trip, huh? And we must have driven all night; otherwise, how would we get so far so fast? I bet we saw some cool stuff."

Like vast plains, mountain ranges, and a night sky filled with more stars than Alexa believed was possible. And a unicorn threatening their lives. Alexa should hate Una for what it had put them through, yet she couldn't. Staying in the present proved difficult when so many memories whirled through her head.

Mateo said, "Do you remember anything else about the lake? Do you have any idea why or how we ended up there?"

The reality was so absurd Alexa laughed. "I might? But it's all just a big mess in my head."

"Like what?"

For his safety, she shouldn't tell him a thing. "When I remember more, I'll let you know. Right now, none of it makes sense. I just want to get through the rest of today."

"Fair enough." Mateo rested his head against Alexa's shoulder. "I'll be here when you need me."

Chapter Thirty-Eight

AS SHE LEFT HER QUIET lunch with Mateo and re-entered the lion's den, a spotlight may as well have shone upon her while wending through the busy halls. Conversations ceased. Voices fell into muffled whispers. Alexa focused her gaze far enough ahead to not run into anyone but avoided eye contact with everyone she passed.

A boy she didn't know waved a hand her way and called out, "Glad to see you're okay."

Alexa bowed her head and murmured a soft "thank you" while clutching the straps of her backpack tighter. She touched the scarf from her sister's closet, checking for the hundredth time if it covered the mess of bruises covering her throat.

"Looking good, Alexa," a big male voice boomed from a doorway.

The voice caught her off-guard. She stopped in her tracks. The flash of a giant man bearing down on her, ham-hands seizing her throat, curdled the food in her gut. She raced to the nearest bathroom and vomited up her lunch.

Would every day be like this? Bouncing between horrible memories while trying to stay sane in her present?

They had little time between classes, so Alexa couldn't linger in the bathroom stall. She flushed the remnants of her lunch, gathered her book bag, and hurried out of the stall. Several inquisitive faces turned her way as she wiped the vomit from her lips, rinsed her mouth, washed her hands, and continued on her way. She plopped into her seat in Psychology class and tried to disappear.

By the time she reached her final period, AP US History, she was both utterly exhausted and jittery with the expectation of seeing Sid again. Alexa arrived as early as possible and was surprised to find most of the class in the room too. Most. Sid hadn't arrived yet.

The faint murmur of conversation halted the moment Alexa entered the classroom.

"Alexa, great to see you." Mr. Hines stood at his desk.

Alexa approached her teacher. "Can we talk about my makeup work after class? I think I missed a test?"

"Of course." Mr. Hines's droning voice, for once, held a prick of emotion. Was he also worried about her? "We'll discuss a time for you to make up the test from last Thursday. How about we figure it out by the end of the week? We're just glad to have you back. And if you need anything, please don't hesitate to ask."

"Thanks, Mr. Hines," Alexa said. Most of the teachers responded similarly, but Mr. Hines's kindness struck deeper than some others. He was a man of few emotions and even less flexibility with late homework and missed tests.

Alexa hurried to her seat and stuffed her hands in her lap. They were already shaking in anticipation of Sid's arrival. The worst thing he could do was ignore her. After everything they had been through, and even though he didn't remember, she wasn't ready to let go of the friendship they had developed.

Finally, surrounded by his posse of soccer chums, Sid entered the classroom. A sharp pulse of need sang through

Alexa's system when their eyes locked. Neither held the other's gaze for more than a second. Sid attempted to make light of the situation by giving Trevon a little grief about something he said at lunch.

Knowing she would see Sid at some point, Alexa had put on her favorite outfit to give her confidence. Her forehead had healed enough that her bangs covered what was left. She had made an effort brushing and styling her hair for once in her life.

Alexa raised her eyes from her textbook when she sensed Sid settling into his assigned seat to her right. She dared not turn his way while all the other students snatched furtive glances. They must have anticipated some kind of reunion but were sorely disappointed.

Mr. Hines called his students to attention, and everyone's focus shifted to their teacher. Today's topic was the War of 1812. Turning to the page Mr. Hines had written on the board, she sensed Sid's eyes upon her. She glanced his way and was caught in his intense gaze. He studied her unapologetically as if searching for some sort of answer.

Sid scratched something onto a loose piece of paper. He folded it once, twice, and when Mr. Hines turned his back, tossed it onto Alexa's desk. She unfolded the note in her lap while Mr. Hines began scrawling the names of British Generals. Sid's jagged scrawl was messier than expected. The note read: *My car, after school?*

Alexa's cheeks burned, and her heart was off to the races. She gave him a quick nod and clutched the paper like a prized possession. She wanted to tell him everything but knew being careful was the better choice. She had no idea what he remembered or his current state of mind.

She jotted down as many notes as her dislocated attention span allowed. When she focused on Mr. Hine's lecture, a random, unwanted memory broke through her concentration. This time, her thoughts focused on the monster—the Brume.

Her notes decomposed into a whirling flurry of haphazard drawings tumbling across her notebook. The lines arched in bulbous swirls. Engrossed in her work, she pressed her pencil too hard, and the lead snapped. The monster's twisted shape writhed around the margin of her notes.

Alexa crumpled her drawing of the Brume as the end-of-day bell sounded. Announcements and calls for students to meet with various individuals piped through the loudspeaker. Alexa stuffed her drawing into the front pocket of her backpack.

Sid jumped up and jogged out of the room before she realized he left. Alexa methodically put the rest of her school supplies into her backpack. Her heart took off again. She was about to go and speak to Sid. Sid who probably remembered nothing. Sid, who had permanently stolen her heart somewhere between Wyoming and the edge of Nevada.

Chapter Thirty-Nine

THE PARKING LOT AT the end of the day was its usually chaos as hundreds of teenage drivers tried to leave the same place at the same time. Alexa texted her mom that Sid had offered to drive her home—an assumption on Alexa's part. If things went badly, a long walk home might be exactly what she needed.

Fine, but you need to be home by 5, Cynthia texted. *I want to know how your day went and discuss what happens now that you're home safe.* Alexa then relayed the same information to Mateo, and he responded in a flurry of wild emojis, including smiley faces and hearts.

Alexa found Sid leaning against the trunk of his Impreza. His thick mop of hair floated in the crisp fall breeze. She saw him before he saw her, and she recognized his tight, nervous expression. She waved to catch his attention.

He smiled, frowned, and shouted, "Get in," before dropping into his driver's seat.

Heart banging like a gong, Alexa tossed her backpack onto the passenger side floor and slid into the seat. Sid's car was spotless compared to hers. Well, her former vehicle. The poor Civic was likely being stripped for parts back in Oregon.

Sid turned on his car, picked out some music, and started backing out of the parking space. The familiar strains of Alice in Chains' "Man in a Box" chugged over the speakers.

"I thought you said you didn't like Alice in Chains," Alexa pointed out. "Too depressing."

Alexa realized her mistake the moment the words left her lips. Before Thursday, she didn't know that Sid preferred old-school hip-hop. She pulled her black denim jacket tighter over her Smashing Pumpkins t-shirt and reached for the stocking cap that wasn't there.

"Yes, they're incredibly depressing." Sid's jaw flexed. "But I can't stop listening to, like, all those bands you have on your t-shirts. Why is that, Alexa?"

She blew the honest answer out between her lips, then lied. "We must have spent a while in my car to get to Oregon. Maybe I played some of my favorite music along the way?"

"Or maybe you also shared a few playlists with me." Sid pursed his lips and turned his car into the line of vehicles leaving the high school parking lot.

"I did?" Alexa played dumb.

"You did."

They reached the parking lot exit. Riverview's version of rush hour sped past. Watching for a gap in traffic, Sid burst out, "Do you remember anything?"

"Um, not really." She turned her flushed face away from him.

"Nothing?" Sid hit the gas and sent the Subaru through a tight seam in the traffic flow. A few horns blared. Alexa squealed, gripping her seat. To her relief, Sid managed to maintain control of the tight turn and joined other commuters without further incident.

"I don't have much time," Sid said as he turned right into a neighborhood along the edge of town. "My parents plan on keeping me under tight surveillance until I head off to college. And they put a tracking app on my phone. Hopefully, they're both too busy with work right now to see I'm taking the long way home."

"The long way?" Alexa said. Rows of pine trees flashed by as they followed a route very familiar to Alexa. "My parents are a mess, too. They don't know what to do with me since I almost—"

"You almost died?" Sid filled in the gap. "What the fuck happened to us, Alexa? All I have is a series of crazy texts on my phone. I was clearly not giving them the whole truth. And I totally ignored my friend's messages, too. Oh, and a cut on my stomach. And your playlists."

Alexa squirmed in her seat. "What was your first memory in Oregon? When did you realize where you were?"

Were they going to Birkmose Park, or was the route a coincidence?

"The first thing I remember is sitting in the back of a police car," Sid said. "I had no idea how I got there and wasn't handcuffed. There were park rangers all over the place, too. I might have started yelling at some point, but no one liked that very much. I saw Mateo, but I couldn't remember his name at the time or what the hell he was doing out there. There was a lake. A rescue crew pulling something up the side of the road. I think it was you. You sure you don't remember anything?"

They took another turn, and Alexa knew precisely where they were going.

What did she remember before the real memories returned? "I remember a lake. I guess that was Crater Lake, huh? I was cold. The sky was huge. And then the next thing I was waking up in a hospital with my mom next to me. Oh, are we going to the park?"

Alexa played dumb as they climbed the steep hill leading to Birkmose Park. One bad snowfall and the park would be closed for the season. Even the park felt different from the last time she was there. The sky hung thick and gray above them, and the threat of rain darkened the horizon on the Minnesota side of the river bluffs.

Sid parked near the bathroom structure. A little too near for Alexa's taste. She quivered in the presence of the cinder-block building's dangerous secret. The Rift only opened one way, and until Una walked through it, the door was a lost part of the intergalactic highway's inventory. A door that could only be found by those who channeled the universe's energy through their flesh. The Brume had wisely locked the Rift behind him when they came through, which put Alexa's mind at ease.

"Why did we come here?" Alexa said. Was the bathroom still a mess? They had left the accessible stall in ruins. She craned her neck to check out the door to the women's bathroom entrance. A wrinkled, paper "Out of Order" sign was hung on the door.

"I don't know." Sid shook his head and scanned the park. "I've had lots of strange feelings since I got home—weird desires to see and do things. I can't stop listening to your playlist. I keep Googling stuff about—now this is going to sound bonkers—unicorns?"

Alexa burst into laughter. Sid didn't know how to respond. At first, he looked hurt, but then he joined her.

"Crazy, right?" Sid broke out his all too familiar crooked grin.

"Sure is," Alexa giggled and pictured Una snorting and bucking across the park.

"And—" Sid swallowed, and his cheeks reddened. "I'm thinking about you a lot."

Alexa also flushed. "Oh, really?"

"I feel this, I don't know, familiarity?"

"Yeah?"

"What do you feel?"

His eyes were so big and deep she could lose herself in them. The gold flecks she noticed while in the Rapid City diner weren't visible in the dim light of a dreary afternoon. Her chest ached. She wanted to tell him everything, but she couldn't. Could she? He would never believe her.

She coughed through the lump in her throat and whispered. "I feel the same as you. Like I know you."

"It's bizarre, right?" Sid studied Alexa.

"Sure is." Alexa could hardly breathe. She wanted him more than ever before. Was that possible? Had things changed?

Sid clasped and unclasped his hands. "Would you maybe hang out with me sometime?"

Alexa traced the shape of his hands with her artist's eyes. She imagined how she would draw his hands in her sketchbook, especially the tiny scar on the knuckle of his right pointer finger. He turned his hand and offered it to her. She accepted. Her stomach flipped, and her cheeks were an inferno. It wasn't quite the romantic grasp of lovers, but it was more than enough for Alexa.

She trilled in her nervous bird voice, "Yeah, sounds good."

"Awesome. We probably can only have lunch together since I'm grounded for life. But maybe we can grab coffee after school sometime?"

Alexa bobbed her head. "That would be great."

The world tipped and spun as he smiled at her, a smile that turned her into a puddle in less than ten seconds. She clutched the hand of the boy she adored for so many years and repeated, "Lunch would be perfect."

About the Author

Theatre professor by day and writer by night, T.J. Fier's other works include the short stories "Kelpie" in *Nothing Short of Horror*, "EVP Session #454" in the September issue of Brilliant Flash Fiction, "The Hunt" in *Tales From the Frozen North: A Winter Anthology*, "Reindeer Games" in *The Colour Out of Deathlehem*, "Hoarfrost" in *Seasons in the Dark* and *Welcome to Effham Falls* which includes her short story, "Heart's Desire." You can also find her @iamfierless on Twitter, and Facebook, and @tjfier_author on Instagram and Threads.

Read more at https://linktr.ee/tjfier.